To P[
All M,
Go Pack Go!
12/15/17

Football in Heaven

MATTHEW NEBEL

ISBN: 1548962414
ISBN-13: 978-1548962418

www.FootballinHeaven.com

For anyone who needs a win after enduring a loss.

PREGAME:
TAKING AN ETERNITY

MATTHEW NEBEL

Several men gather on a tiny midwestern field. Nothing but the eternity of space is above them, and the glossy light of the moon polishes their heads. Icicles glisten on the grass like a meadow of diamonds. A man takes the smallest step and sends a cluster of them shattering to the ground. Little wisps of breath can be seen puffing from each throat, and the men huddle together, shivering to keep warm. It's the coldest night of the year.

Why do they gather in this way? Why would anyone endure this cold on purpose?

The men look at each other. Each person knows exactly why he's here. Each person has his specific purpose. All of them have the same goal.

Suddenly the ground shakes. Then again, making the men forget about the cold. Through the dark green forest, the towering enemies can be seen approaching. Moonlit shadows, one hundred feet long, are cast like a drape over the men. Every step from one of the giants sends an echo into the night, and all together, they sound like a band of drums. The lead giant is the first to set foot on the open field. He stares downward at the huddled men, who suddenly feel like tiny icicles about to be shattered.

Then hope arrives. The leader of the men emerges from the other edge of the field. The men turn, and they all feel a shimmer of solace, because he will tell them exactly what to do. The man sprints to them. He quickly tells them not to worry, that it will all be all right. He tells them even the tallest giant can be slain if they have faith in their team. With unmatched authority, he shouts the game plan, telling each where to go and what to do. They split into battle formation. Each man will face his own giant alone, but together they will fight as one team.

The moon above them explodes into a cluster of lights that scatter and flood the entire field. Thousands of spectators materialize, calling for bloodshed.

The ball is placed, the whistle blows, and the final battle begins.

"Down, set, hut!" The words come from the quarterback of the Green Bay Packers. His name is Gordon Fisher, and he takes the ball from his lineman, knowing with every fiber of his being that every action has a consequence. He takes a fraction of a second to think about the past two decades. All the decisions he's made in his entire career—all the consequences—have accumulated in him standing right here on the north end of Lambeau Field, the battle arena that his team calls home. Soon he might not be standing here. Maybe he will be or maybe he won't, because another fraction of a second will cause another decision that will cause another consequence.

That fraction of a second passes by, he drops back a few yards, and his linemen begin their attempt to stave off the New York Giants defense. He's no longer thinking about his past. He's thinking about his present. He checks for his wide receiver, and sees him being covered by a defender step-for-step down field. Gordon decides against it for now—he'll check back on him later. A Giants' defensive end loops around the back, and Gordon dodges forward. He's now fully encircled by his teammates.

He's counting on them. He's trusting that each one can slay his own Giant.

Another fraction of a second passes, and his running back breaks into the open field. Gordon chooses not to throw to him either. He sees his wide receiver cut back outside at the 45-yard line, trying to shed his defender off his route. Another fraction of a second passes and Gordon needs to make a decision. His arm bends back like a sling, then he swings it forward.

As the ball floats through the two decades it took to get there, Gordon takes a second to think about his career and his life. There were so many decisions and so many consequences. Perhaps this will be the final decision. Perhaps there will be one more. All he knows is that he can never have this one back. The ball revolves slowly. It is a clock, and the laces are the second hand, ticking away the little amount of time each person has left. Finally, the air beneath the ball shatters, and it drops clean out of the sky. Gordon is no longer thinking about the present. He is thinking about the future.

MATTHEW NEBEL

1ST QUARTER:
LAYING THE BLUEPRINTS

1

"Interception!"

I scream the words to the sky. I tuck the football in my right arm and take off. No one is ahead of me. The wind rips my breath away, but I keep just enough energy to break free into the end zone. I hold up the ball like a trophy. Touchdown—the greatest feeling in the world. It's like the sun breaking through the clouds on a cold day.

I turn back to the field, and I realize that my touchdown was nothing to brag about. Two other ten-year-olds, my friends Jared and Randy, are the only other kids on the field. I could have just as easily dodged a dolphin in a desert.

"What were you thinking?" Jared yells at Randy.

"What do you mean? You got the ball picked off."

"Yeah, from your crappy throw. I was wide open."

"You were not. Victor practically had a leash on you."

"Oh yeah? Well if I wasn't even open, then why did you throw me the ball?"

Randy points at two younger girls over on the monkey bars. "I figured one of them could have gotten to it first. They look a hell of a lot quicker than you."

Randy shoves Jared with his elbow, and gets pushed back. I just stay there and wait for them to settle down.

The sun is gone now, and the crickets have started humming. I take a breath of cool air through my nose. "Guys," I say, "It's late. I need to be home."

"It's only eight," Randy says. But I just shrug my shoulders at both of them and say nothing. Randy huffs, "All right dude. Same time tomorrow?"

"Uhh, can't tomorrow. I got other plans," I say.

"What're you doing?" Jared says.

"Nothing." I flip him the football.

"Well, don't avoid us forever," he says, "It's not like we have a lot of days left."

Randy shoots him a look, and I pretend not to notice. Jared quickly covers his tracks. "I meant days left in the summer," he says, "before school starts, and before the season starts. That's all I meant, Vic."

"No, it's okay . . . honestly." I take a few seconds, then turn and wave goodbye. Behind me, I hear the two of them mumbling about something not related to football.

Green Bay, Wisconsin, is called a small city, but it's really more like a big town. Growing up in Green Bay, you see a lot of the same people wherever you go, and most people never feel like they need to leave. It's like a sweater that was knitted by your grandma—it may be old and worn down, but it's not going to fall apart.

But when outsiders think of Green Bay, they think of football. More specifically, they think of the Packers. That's because the town owns the team, and it's the only pro team like that in the whole country. So half the businesses in the phonebook are called Packerland, or something like that.

I was born in 1997, right after the Packers last won the Super Bowl. A decade later, we still haven't won any big games, but I love cheering for the team. It feels like cheering for my own family.

That's all to say that on Sundays, most people go to two temples. The most important is church, and right there next to it is Lambeau Field. As you pass through the town on the highway, you can see the green walls reach above the one-story houses that surround it. Up close, it looks more like a green castle on top of a hill, keeping watch on its village. I bike past this castle every day, and it really does make me feel protected.

A few blocks away from the stadium, I pull my bike up onto the curb of my apartment. The yellowing light bulb above our front door buzzes. I open the rusty front door, and the hinges scream.

Mom comes bounding around the corner as soon as I'm in the living room. The floor creaks beneath the carpet with every step. When she sees me standing there, there's a quick pause that lasts long enough for me to know what's coming, but short enough that I have no time to hide.

"Go to your room. Right now."

"I was just—"

"That's the third night in a row. No more excuses!"

"I was at the park. With Randy and Jared."

"What did I just say?"

She points toward the hallway, as if I need help finding my way. I keep my eyes low and turn down the hallway to the first door on the right. I kick my desk chair out of the way and step over a stack of papers on my floor before falling onto my bed. There's a lonely pit in my stomach. It's the feeling that comes when a person you care about is disappointed in you. What makes it worse is when you know you've done nothing wrong.

A bird squawks outside my window. I can feel my hair matted to the side of my head. There's no noise coming from the kitchen, and by the light outside I'm guessing it's only about six or seven in the morning

The sleep in my eyes is still fresh and gross. I sit up and turn myself over so that my legs are dangling off the bed and my feet are hovering inches above the floor. The floorboard creaks as I ease my way to a stand.

I notice a plate of rice and pork chops teetering on my desk. Mom probably brought it in last night while I was sleeping. It isn't really like her to get angry the way she did. Normally if I came home when I did last night, she'd ask me what I was thinking coming home so early, and practically punt me back out the door. Lately, I think she's just been a bit scared—because of what happened.

It's stuffy, so I slide the small window next to my bed open, and a breeze rushes through.

On the floor is a mountain range of old papers and art projects from school. I had pulled it out from under my bed trying to find one specific sheet of paper, but I don't even know if it got shuffled into the mix. Finding it is my first task for today.

The first paper on the stack is a painting I made in art class a couple years ago. It shows a small cabin up north. There's a patch of smoke coming from the chimney, with the entire lawn wrapped with thick red leaves from the surrounding trees. It makes me feel a weird soup of emotions. It's not that the painting is so well painted. I think it's because the fall season is such a weird time of year—it's pretty and calm, but the only reason it's there is to move us into winter.

I set the painting aside for now, and don't know if I'll ever care to look at it again for as long as I just did. I turn my attention to a stack of language arts papers.

On top is one of the first real essays I ever wrote, titled "My Best Friend Tyler." I skim over it, and toss it to the side. Then the next sheet on the pile makes me stop breathing.

It's a single leaf of paper, crinkled and worn, like a faded memory. The title reads "Things I want to do before I die." I started it a long time ago as a little activity in school, but I took it home with me and kept adding stuff here and there whenever I thought of something good. The list grew to about thirty things, some of them for real and some as jokes (for instance, I don't ever imagine myself actually skateboarding on the moon).

But after some time, the paper got lost under my bed. It's been there ever since, crumpled and abandoned with my stuffed bear and city of Legos.

I run my finger through all the lines, starting at the bottom, and I draw a few mental check marks on some of the entries. *Eat an entire box of Oreos. Go to a PG-13 movie alone. Go skydiving*—I haven't done that one yet. I don't know if they even let ten-year-olds go skydiving.

Then I come to the top. The first thing on my list: *Take the Packers to the Super Bowl.* If they made a plaque to remember my childhood, that would be the quote. When I was younger, Dad always told me I'd be the next Gordon Fisher. He would take me out back, and we'd play catch until after dark, when we couldn't even see the ball anymore and we were only guessing where to stretch our arms out for a catch.

For a long time, he had me convinced that I would take the Packers to the big game. But now I know that it will never happen.

I stare at the list, and think back.

It was a few weeks ago when everything started. I was helping Dad carry some groceries into the apartment. Then, all of a sudden, the sun filled my eyes, and it felt like it was the only thing that existed. I heard Dad shouting for me, but he sounded like he was really far away, and I fell on the ground.

They took me to the hospital, but I don't remember much. I remember crying for Mom and asking if everything was going to be okay. But she couldn't hear me because by then it felt like she was fading away.

When the noise ended, I was in a room that was like an endless hallway with a hundred million other people that I realized looked a lot like me. Soon, I started to remember who I was and what I was. I was a human, my name was Victor Ross, and I lived in an apartment with my mom and dad.

"What happened?" I said.

Dad hesitated. "You just . . . fell."

Dad turned to Mom, but Mom was already looking away. After a few seconds, he kneeled down next to my hospital bed. His eyes were quivering.

"Is everything okay?" I asked.

Then, just like Mom, he turned away, too.

And that's when I knew that I was done.

"Cardiomyopathy" is the word Dr. McKenzie told me. He said it over and over again. Car-dee-oh-my-ah-pa-thee. So that I would remember the thing that was trying to harm me.

"Cardiomyopathy," he told me, "means your heart has trouble pumping blood to the rest of your body. That's why you fainted."

He went on to explain that cardiomyopathy—as bad as I have it—is only curable through a heart transplant, and the waiting list was longer than a miracle could even fix.

As I lay there in my hospital bed, I listened to the doctor talk about my life like I wasn't even a person. Like I was just on his clipboard. He spoke in really long words that I didn't understand, but I picked up the gist of what he said: the disease would do its best to make me and everyone around me as sad as possible. Then, after it was absolutely sure it had done that, it would kill me.

Mom and Dad never looked at me that entire time. That night, we stayed up late, praying to God that he would help us find a transplant. But even then, I felt like they were praying for me instead of with me. I wasn't sure if my prayers were even being heard. It felt cold and lonely, like I was in a storm without a coat.

It's been weeks now since I got out of the hospital, and I still haven't really seen the Mom and Dad that I used to know. It's weird, like they're behind a wall that can filter out anything they don't feel like hearing. And that's why things are weird around here lately.

But anyway, that's all to say that I won't be taking the Packers to the championship. So what? Thinking back, it's kind of a funny thought to begin with. Millions of kids grow up and never get to play pro football. And according to the doctors, I might not even have until Christmas. That's barely long enough for me to keep playing peewee football this fall.

But the list can wait for now. It isn't even what I'm supposed to be looking for. I turn my attention back to the pile of paper. A few papers down, I finally find it. The paper is a little crinkled, with brown water stains on some of the corners. I feel a slight jump in my heart.

Then, I get an idea. I crawl to the corner and snatch back the "wish list," fold it out and rub the creases flat on my knee. I take the pen from the floor and squeeze in one last entry at the bottom. *Win the race with Tyler.* I draw an empty check box to the left. Then I slide my hand in between my bed's top and bottom mattresses and slip the list in the middle.

In the living room, Mom is reading the paper on the couch. I don't know where Dad is. I sneak past the living room into the kitchen and snag the cordless phone off the hook.

"Hello?" A sweet voice answers on the other end. It's Tyler's mom, Sarah.

"Hey, is Tyler there?" I say.

"Oh, hey there Victor. He's outside right now, I'll go get him."

"No, that's okay. Just let him know I'm on my way over."

"Okay, Vic."

"Thanks."

"Bye-bye."

I set off back through the living room and open up the front hall closet. As I clamber for my shoes, Mom finally says, "Where are you headed off to?"

"Tyler's house. Gonna be there all day."

"Don't stay there too late."

I scoff, but I pass it off as me struggling to slip on my left shoe. I yank the Velcro strap tight. "I won't," I say. "I'll be back before it gets dark." I get up and open the door.

"Wait!" she yells.

"What?" I say. What could she possibly need now that she couldn't have already asked me?

"The phone," she says. "Leave the phone here. Please."

I look down. The cordless phone is still in my hand. I slam it down on the side table, and leave with a huff. I know she's right, but I guess I kind of wanted her to feel like she was wrong.

I burst out the door and cover my ears as the door squeaks. Finally I grab my bike off the railing and set off down Oneida Street with the soapbox-racer plans sitting tightly in my pocket.

Tyler's parents are friends with my parents, so I've known him since before I can remember. Because he's about a year and a half younger—two grades lower—I tend to get a lot of crap from my other friends for hanging out with him. He's an easy target because he's so tiny. Like, really tiny. He's going into third grade, but he wears hand-me-downs from when I was in kindergarten.

Tyler is waiting for me in his driveway with the garage door open. As soon as I show him the blueprints, he snaps them out of my hand and brushes his long, black bangs out of his eyes to take a better look.

"It took me forever to find," I say.

He rubs the creases between his fingers. "Where was it?"

"Under my bed. I was cleaning out my room and stumbled over it. Thought you'd want to see it."

"Yeah . . . I've been hoping for something like this," he says.

"Like what?" I ask.

"You know, something you and me can work on together, before . . ." He looks away and tries to hide his face, just like my parents.

"Yeah, me too," I say quickly. "Can't wait."

The door to the garage opens, and Sarah carries a tray with lemonade and cookies over the threshold. "Well hey, Victor! How've you been doing?"

"Great," I say. "I was just showing Tyler the plans I found. We're going to build a soapbox racer and drive it in the race this fall."

"Oh, that's wonderful. You guys will have so much fun." She sets the tray down on top of a cooler and leans over Tyler to see. Tyler is a little hesitant to show her. His parents are a little nosy, so he likes to keep anything he can to himself. But he finally shows her, and she says, "Well that's just wonderful! You boys will have so much fun." Then she turns and walks back into the house.

I turn to Tyler. "Well if you're serious about doing this," I say, "we're going to have to get started. We've only got a few months."

"Whad'ya mean?" he blurts. Then I realize what I just said.

"No, I mean a few months left until the tournament. It's in November."

"Oh," he says plainly.

"We're gonna win this thing," I say.

He smiles. "Yeah we are."

We toast with our lemonade, and twist open a package of Oreos. The afternoon floats by while we lie on the floor of the garage and plan out how the racer will look. We copy some of the plans onto sheets of white paper and sketch out designs of how we want to paint it. I put a jet engine on the back of one of mine, and Tyler jokes that we might get a bird caught in it.

In the afternoon, a BMW rolls into the driveway and out pops Tyler's dad, Mike, in his shining white collar.

"What's up dudes?" he says in a pretend surfer voice. Mike is always cheery, like Sarah. After a minute, he goes inside to change his clothes, and drives us down to Menards to get some lumber.

Later, back at Tyler's dinner table, I get a heavy helping of chop suey thwopped on my plate. His mom makes a nice dinner, and always wants me to have the biggest share.

"So, school's coming up pretty soon, eh boys?" Mike says.

"Yeah," Tyler sighs.

"So Victor," he asks me, "who's the lucky teacher that gets to bring out the paddle this year?"

"Ms. Sherman," I say, "and I don't think she has a paddle."

"Well, she'd better have a ruler, at least."

Tyler looks down at his plate, and I give a little laugh to let Mike know I get the joke.

"So what's the official countdown?" Mike says. "Nine days?"

"Ten days," Tyler says. He looks at me.

21

"We've both agreed that we don't want to mention it anymore," I say. I take in another mouthful. Tyler gets a nod from his dad.

"So who's taking him clothes shopping?" he says.

"I will," Sarah says. "We'll go on Monday."

"He can't go Monday, he's coming fishing with us, remember?"

Tyler suddenly looks down again. Ah, the yearly fishing trip. I know the pain. Each year, Tyler's dad and uncles take him out on Lake Michigan for a few days. It sounds great at first, but Tyler hates every minute of it. I know because I went with him once.

"You're welcome to join us, you know," Mike offers me. As appealing as it sounds—sitting quietly, listening to his uncles' drunken rants, all while getting sunburned and seasick—I don't really want to go. Tyler promised after last year that he'd never make me go again.

"He can't," Tyler says. "He's . . . busy." Everyone turns my way, and I'm a deer in headlights. "He's got a checkup this week."

As quickly as they looked at me, they look away, as though their mashed potatoes have suddenly become more interesting.

I quickly say, "It's just a routine checkup. I'm feeling great lately."

"Well, we'll keep you in our prayers, then," Sarah says.

After the moment passes, Mike asks, "So do you have anything fun going on this week, while you're at it?"

"Yeah," I say, "I'm actually going to training camp on Monday. To watch the Packers."

"Really?" Mike asks. "That's great."

"Yeah," I say.

"Are you bringing your bike?" Sarah asks.

"Yeah."

"Good boy. Tyler almost got a player to ride his last year."

"Yeah. Well, I'm not counting on it."

"You see the game Friday, Victor? Heck of a hit."

I know which hit he means instantly. "Yeah. Nasty," I say. In the last preseason game, our wide receiver Sean Driver got smashed into the ground trying to shake off some defenders. He had to get carted off the field.

"Could be a sprained ankle. Pretty bad. Hope he's not out."

"I'm sure he'll be fine," I say. "Sean's tough. He knows how to take a hit."

"Well, you'd better say hi to him for us on Monday, then. Wish him well," Sarah smiles.

"I will." I smile stupidly.

I take another scoopful of food on my fork. My mind is still on other things. On the doctor's visit. On the fact that nobody will talk to me about it. After stopping for a second with the food dangling in front of me, I plunge it into my mouth.

I figure if I'm not going to be doing any talking, I might as well make it look like my mouth is busy.

It's late now, and the front windows of Tyler's house reflect the sun. Sarah is sending me home with a large Tupperware tub full of chop suey. I think she made extra knowing that I'd take some with me. She knows how things are at home these days. My family and me, we're accepting all the chop suey we can get.

I turn my bike back onto Oneida Street, and I see Lambeau Field again. This time it's not a castle; it's just a wall splitting the city into two separate parts. Tyler's family is on one side, and mine is on the other.

Dad is a teacher, so he makes regular money, but not a lot, especially compared with Mike.

Mom is an electrician. She learned the trade from her dad, and she's been at it ever since. There aren't a lot of women electricians, so I think that's pretty cool.

I look at the stadium again, and focus on one of lights along a stairwell just inside.

Mom was one of the people who headed the electrical team during the stadium renovations a few years ago. It was a huge deal for us, and I kind of like to show it off to my friends. I point at the stadium and tell them that those lights are ours. Every time I see them, I think of her and how hard she worked.

These days, no one is hiring, and the work is about as hard as the sofa she spends most her days on. She says it's part of the business; highs and lows. She'll find a job soon, she says.

That's why I'm biking home from Tyler's house. See, we used to live right across the street from him. That's how our families met. That's how Tyler and I became friends. And God must have blessed us both that it happened that way, because if it didn't, I'd probably be one of the punks picking on him at school.

But when Mom lost her job, we had to move out of our house. Tyler's family invited us into their house to stay until we found a place of our own. Ever since then, it's kind of been hard between our parents. Mine always feel guilty whenever we're around his, like we owe them something and we can never pay them back.

Now, we live on the other side of Lambeau Field, in an apartment where the porch light buzzes and flickers, and the screen door screams in pain when it's opened. If you saw the place with your own eyes, you'd swear that the brick walls were even rusted.

It's nighttime when I slip inside. No one is home yet. I set the Tupperware down on the kitchen table and can't help but notice the electrical bill lying out. At least someone is making Mom's money.

I microwave the chop suey, and then I plunge the fork in and sigh a long sigh. The legs on the table are uneven, and they start to wobble. I watch the light bulb above me flickering dim. I know how it feels.

2

I'm standing outside the gates of Lambeau Field, somewhere near the back of a crowd of hundreds of kids my age. I thought I'd be the only one out here because of the near downpour of rain. But everyone around me has their parents holding umbrellas over them. All I have is my one and only Packer hat, but even that isn't helping block the rain. The brim is completely chopped up from the time Tyler attacked it with a pair of scissors. He was four years old at the time, so I couldn't get mad at him.

I look up with my mouth open, trying to catch a few raindrops. Then I hear what I've been waiting for. The crowd starts to cheer.

Every day during summer training camp, kids bring their bikes with them and let the players ride them from the stadium to the practice field. These days you have to get lucky though, because everybody wants in on the action.

The gate opens, and a few of the staff and some new players walk out. I recognize the new kicker—Number 2; I forget what his name is. Then a few other guys I don't recognize jump onto some kids' bikes and head off down the parking lot hill. One of the kids my age gets picked, and his face brightens with joy as the player three times his size straddles his bike. I see he can barely even bend his knees enough to fit on the seat, but he shrugs it off and hands the kid his helmet, both of them beaming. They both take off down the hill, tires spewing puddles of water aside while the small pair of shoes clop along behind.

The crowd thins, and I try to push through to the front. More players head out as the minutes go by. Then, behind us, a large black SUV peels around the corner of the stadium. Inside is a bulky man with a chiseled jaw and short beard. Everyone cranks their heads around to look.

"Who's that?" a kid asks his dad, pulling at the waist of his jeans.

"I think that's Gordon," he responds, and he snaps his camera.

"Really?" the kid lights up. "Gordon Fisher?"

I keep my composure and only laugh to myself. Sure, Gordon is everyone's favorite player—even mine—but he never rides bikes to practice. It would attract way too much attention. I briefly imagine what it would be like if I waited outside the gate with a Ferrari. "Would you like to take this to practice, Mr. Fisher?" I'd ask coolly. Both of us would hop in and throw on some slick shades, so we can look cool for the quarter-mile journey across the parking lot.

I turn my head back to the tunnel, and when the car passes, everyone else does the same. Several more unknown players pass through the tunnel and take a few other bikes off the market. Then I glance back to the entrance of the tunnel to see someone I wasn't expecting at all. A tall wide receiver steps through into the fresh, rainy air. It's Sean Driver, and he's standing on his own. The crowd lets out a giant roar of approval, and I cheer along.

Dad always says that Sean is his favorite player because he never gives up, even at the last second. Sean fought his way into the league after nearly getting fired his first season. Now, he might be one of the best Packers ever.

He strolls through the long path of fans, shining his trademark white smile, which sticks out against his dark skin. He stops every so often to chat with a fan, or sign a kid's T-shirt with his name and his favorite Bible verse. But after all that's over, he scans the crowd and makes his ultimate decision. It's a little girl dressed head to toe in Packer gear that her parents probably slapped on her this morning against her will. She's holding a mountain bike that's as tall as she is. It's pathetic, but Sean can't pass it up.

A few minutes after the practice begins, I lean my bike against the stadium wall and take a seat with my hands in my lap. I reach into my left pocket for a pack of candy that's half-empty and start munching like I'm a stray dog with nowhere to go. I toss the wrapper and watch it as the wind blows it straight to the pavement a few feet away.

Then, as if from the sky, a giant shoe stomps down on the wrapper. I look up, and after I see who it belongs to, I swear my head spins a full circle.

"You want me to throw this away for you?" he says. I don't answer. Not because I'm scared—I would be scared, but he's smiling, so I know it's okay. The reason I don't answer is because I'm looking straight at Sean Driver. My heart jolts into overdrive, and I start to get really hot. I don't know if I'm dreaming or not, but I keep quiet so that I don't say anything stupid—advice I learned from Tyler.

"Don't worry, I got you covered," he says.

I manage to eke out the words, "H-Hello, Mr. Driver," but I say it like a kindergartener going to his first day of school.

"Call me Sean," he says, grabbing the plastic. "What you doing down there?"

"Oh . . . er, I was just sitting," I say.

He offers one of his massive hands, and I reach mine up to be devoured.

"Nice place to sit," he says.

"Um, yeah." I stare for a few more seconds. So many of my friends would have lists of things to say in this situation, but I've got nothing. There has never been a more awkward moment in my life, me sitting here in the glow of his spotless grin. I can tell he's trying to be nice, just waiting for me like all fifty thousand of his other biggest fans.

Finally, I think of something brilliant to say. "So, what are you doing up here?"

"Hah, good question." He keeps smiling and looks down. I follow his gaze, which leads me to see the problem. The same left shoe that flattened my candy wrapper was laced around Sean's right foot. He had two left shoes on.

"I don't know what the deal was," he says. "I put the shoes on when I got to the field. It felt fine right up until coach had us doing stretches. He told us to lift up our left leg, and I fell right out of the air."

I giggle loudly, picturing Sean plunging to the ground like Wile E. Coyote off a cliff.

"So why didn't you just have a trainer come get it for you?" I ask.

"The team made me walk back here like this, so that they could get a good laugh."

He chuckles a little, but then he leans down close and places his hand on my shoulder so that he knows I'm paying attention—as if I'm not. "Really," he says, "I chose to walk back, because it was my fault. Just cause I get paid to play football, that doesn't mean I can forget how to tie my own shoes."

I know what he means when he says this. He wasn't always a pro football player. Before that, he made his own meals, worked hard for much less money, and he probably tied his own shoes. I feel sort of ashamed that I'm wearing Velcro.

"So what's your name, young man?" he asks. I know exactly what's coming next, because he uses the same voice on every other fan he's about to give an autograph to. But I don't want to let him off that easy. I grab my bike from the wall before I answer, accidentally shaking his hand off my shoulder.

"Er, Victor. My name's Victor," I say as I gather myself.

"Victor, huh? So where're your parents at?"

"My dad's running errands. My mom just lost her job and—" I stop myself. I realize I don't need to say that. I shrug nervously. "They know I'm here. I come here all the time," I reassure him. "Never, uh . . . never gotten anyone to ride my bike though." I'm obvious as heck.

"Well that's a shame," he says to let me know he gets the hint. "Let me go fix my problem, and then we'll see if we can fix yours."

"O—okay."

He keeps smiling and then turns into the tunnel, limping every other step until he's out of view.

On the bike, now, we're riding down the parking lot incline toward the practice field; Sean on the pedals and me on the back pegs, gripping only his jersey as the shoulder pads beneath it are too large and too slick for my hands to keep a hold of them.

"So you live close by, then?" he shouts. The wind whips my hair, and I can barely hear him, but none of that matters to me.

"Yeah, just down the street. How'd you know that?"

"You said you come here all the time. I don't imagine you commute from Milwaukee on this bike every day?"

"No," I shrug. I don't even know what commute means. "I live just a couple of blocks down that way."

"I'm sure you've been to a good number of games then."

"Not really," I confess. "I've only been to a couple of scrimmage games. Never a real one, though."

"Well that's too bad. We could use a fan like you on game days. Are you on the waiting list?"

I swallow hard. I'm actually on two waiting lists. The one Sean means is the Packer season ticket waiting list. There are more names on the list right now than there are seats in the stadium, and it grows bigger each year.

"Yeah, I'm on the list," I say. "Probably not gonna happen, though."

"I'm sure you'll make it soon enough."

I swallow again. "Well . . . I might not be around much longer."

"Moving out of town?"

"No. I'm not moving."

He doesn't say anything back. I wonder if he's one of those people Mom and Dad talk about. They say there are some people I can tell, but most people just don't need to know.

"I'm sick," I say. "I might not be around anywhere much longer."

My words zap away the electricity of our conversation. The buzz of distant fans fades to nothing. For the moment, there's only us, the bike, and an ocean of pavement. I can tell he's thinking over what to say to that. I know he wasn't expecting to hear it, or to talk about it. Now I really do wish I hadn't said anything.

"You're—you're sick, huh?"

"Yeah, I am."

"I'm sorry to hear that," he says. Most people try to overreact. But in the end those people just look silly. I learned the word condescending when I became sick. That's what happens when you tell a grown-up you're dying, and they act like you don't even understand what that means—even though you're the one who just told them. They treat you as though, because you're just ten, you haven't been lying in bed each night thinking about the actual meaning of your own life. They treat you like you've just come home for the very first time and you're not even housebroken. They're an owner talking to their puppy.

"You don't have to be sorry," I say. "I mean that, too. I'm getting sick of people doing that."

He doesn't respond.

"I mean—I'm getting tired of that."

The buzz of the fans starts coming back into my ears, and I realize we're getting close to the practice field. Sean pulls into a little walkway behind the field where fans aren't normally allowed to go, and he finally skids the bike to a halt. Still, he doesn't say anything. I wonder if anyone else knows what it feels like to make one of their idols afraid to talk to them.

We both get off, and he hands me the bike. I clutch the handlebars tightly now. They feel warm, like they had just been held by a king.

"Well anyway, thanks for the ride, Sean."

"Uh—yeah. Not a problem." He jerks out of a little stupor, and his face molds into his trademark grin, but it doesn't stretch from ear to ear and his teeth don't sparkle.

"Hey listen," he says to me, "I know you don't want to talk about it right now. It must get really tiring. But I also know it's really scary."

I shuffle uneasily. It's hard to listen to someone talk to you that way. It's even harder when the person that's talking is the one person you dreamed you would only ever talk to if there were some kind of celebration going on. One of my favorite football players is staring at me right now. How is he the one saying this stuff?

He goes on. "But you need to know that God sends you through these times for a reason."

A reason, he says? And he says "through these times" as if I'm going to come out better on the other end.

"Let me explain," he says. "People are going to try to make you feel comfortable; like you're some kind of big hero. But you're not a hero unless you make yourself one."

Suddenly, I realize Sean isn't talking to his puppy anymore.

"You keep changing throughout your entire life," he says, "every last minute of it—and it's your decision whether you're going to grow or shrink."

"I . . . guess you're right," I say.

"It's true, Victor. You need to grow—in strength and in courage. And if you decide to, I have a feeling you can change the world for the better."

I shrug.

"You don't believe that?"

"Yeah, I do . . . I guess."

"Victor, even the smallest change can make a whole world of difference. When you do believe that, I'll know I've done my part."

There's another pause, but it's not an awkward one. I'm just going over these things in my head. It's a moment before I realize he's waiting for me to speak.

"All right, I believe you, Sean."

"Good," he says, and he relaxes his voice a little. "So, do you want me to autograph anything for you?"

What a question. No, not today, Sean. The clothes I've worn are already so full of Sharpie ink from other athletes that there simply isn't any room left.

"Yeah!" I say, and I twist the hat off my head. He takes the brim in his hand and holds it back at arm's length. The brim—jagged, like a shark bite—has him curious.

"My friend did that," I say, and my face goes red. "He cut it up with a pair of scissors. That's why it looks that way."

"I think it's cool," he says, and I wonder why I was worried to begin with. I hand him the Sharpie I had in my pocket, and he shakes it a few times in his hand. "So what did you say your name was, again?"

"Victor," I say.

"No, I mean your full name."

"Just Victor is fine."

"C'mon, it'll make it more genuine."

But I disagree. It makes it less genuine—like we don't know each other. You don't usually call your friend by their full name.

I figure arguing would only make it worse though, so I tell him my name is Victor Ross, and he starts scribbling on my hat. Once he's done he hands it back, and as he does, a ray of sunshine seeps in through the clouds, just in time to ping off of every last one of his teeth as his mouth spreads into a sparkly grin.

"Thanks a lot," I say as he's getting set to head into practice. There's nothing else left to do, so I say, "I'll—I'll see you later, Sean!"

"I'm sure you will," he smiles, turns and steps through the gate. I stand there in his wake and glance downward. I turn the hat over in my hands and read his message: "To Victor, Keep the faith! 2 Tim 4:7" I look up to speak, but by then, he's already in the team huddle.

He didn't write my last name, but I know he was in a hurry, and I'm not the most important person in his life. I'll let it slide.

I smile, hop on my bike, and turn out of the walkway before speeding the entire ride home. The rain is clearing up.

I burst through the front door and into the front hall, the autographed hat clenched tightly in my left hand. "Dad! Dad! Dad!" I shout.

"Dad is out by the car," I hear Mom yell from the kitchen. She adds on, "Why are you back so early? Is something the matter?" but I'm already halfway back out the door before she finishes. Dad is in the parking lot around the side of the building with the hood up on his car and grease stains on his shirt.

"Dad!" I yell, waving my hat high by the brim. "Guess what!"

He turns around. "You made the team?"

"No, even better," I say. I land far too close to him, and I make a pedestal for the hat out of my hands. The Sharpie is still wet, and the name on it sparkles in a ray of sunshine peering through the clouds. He wipes his hand clean with a rag and takes the hat. The corner of his mouth twitches upward.

"I got Sean to ride my bike, Dad."

"You did? Well I'll be." He barely mutters the words when an older man steps over from the other side of the lot. It's our neighbor, Carl. "Whatcha got there, Vic?" he grunts.

Dad answers, "Take a look for yourself, Carl. My boy here made a new friend today." He holds up the hat like a trophy, and I feel like a million bucks.

Mom comes walking around the corner wall. "How did this happen?" she asks. "I thought he was hurt!"

"He got better," I grin.

"No kidding," Dad says. "How'd he handle your wheels?"

"I think he did okay."

"Is that really Driver?" Mom says. "You got to meet him?" There's more pep in her voice than I've heard in a long time.

"Yeah, it's him!" I say.

"Well," she says, "this is amazing. We might have to celebrate."

I smile, but then I remember something else, "I'll be right back out," I say. As soon as I dart across the front lawn for the porch, Mom yells after me. "Where are you headed?"

"Gotta tell Tyler!" I say. But then I remember before she even responds.

"He's on his fishing trip, remember?"

I skid to a halt. "Oh yeah," I say. And just like that, the fire inside me flickers down.

"He'll be back in a few days. You can tell him first thing."

I stand there for a moment. Okay, I can keep the fire burning until then.

3

A young nurse calls my name. She looks like a nice babysitter, which is probably a reason they hired her. She takes me and Mom back into the checkup room where Dr. McKenzie is waiting.

"Hey there, Victor," he says.

He sits down with his clipboard and brings himself to eye level with me sitting on the table-bed thing. He flashes a smile. "How we doing today, buddy?"

"Good," I say.

"Good, good." He shuffles through the pages on his clipboard.

"So what we're doing here today," he says to both of us, "is just evaluating the situation. We want to see how Victor's body is handling itself. Now, Victor, you've said that you've been feeling fine lately, is that correct?"

I give a full nod.

"Kay. Good, that's good." He glances down at his chart. "So even though you're feeling okay on the outside, we're going to have to run a few more tests to make sure you're feeling okay on the inside."

The machines they have me hooked up to this time are smaller and less scary than the ones they had before—the ones that tried to swallow me. But Mom is still worried. Back in the waiting room, after the tests are done, she barely even talks to me. She just grips the chair and looks out the window.

"Victor?" The nurse calls my name, and we follow her into the patient room. Mom lags behind a little in the hallway.

"It's fine," I tell her.

We take our seats in the patient room, and Dr. McKenzie is waiting for us. He takes out his usual clipboard and clicks out the pen.

"First things first," he says. "We're looking pretty good. In all honesty, Victor's looking better than we had been expecting."

Mom doesn't say anything—if she did, she would be admitting that anything else was even possible.

"But with that said," he says, "the transplant waiting list is still very long. If nothing changes, he'll still be at a high risk. We're still going to have to keep a close eye on him going into this school year."

Suddenly, I feel my left hand clenching, and I realize that Mom has been holding it this whole time, pinning it to the armrest without knowing it. It hurts, but I don't want her to think she's hurting me, so I grip the other armrest with my right hand to keep my mind off of it.

Dr. McKenzie goes on. "Victor can definitely go to school, as normal, but I must insist that he be taken out at the first sign of alarm, just as a precautionary measure."

"That's fine," I say more to Mom than to Dr. McKenzie. I try to be as happy-sounding as I can, for her sake.

"I'm good as long as I can hang out with my friends," I say, "and play football."

"You're signed up for football?" he asks.

"Yeah, it's my first year of tackle."

"I see."

He doesn't say anything else. He just looks down at his clipboard, and my fake smile fades away.

"Is everything all right?" I say.

"Victor, I can't recommend that you play football in your condition."

"But you just said I was fine."

"I know, Victor, but we're looking out for your safety here."

"It's not your body, it's mine. You can't stop me from playing if I want to." I turn my head to Mom, as if she has some sort of an answer.

"Isn't there any other option?" she says.

"We're only looking out for Victor's safety, I can assure you."

"It's just that football means a lot to him. You have to understand."

Dr. McKenzie just looks at his stupid clipboard. He doesn't even look Mom in the eye. And Mom won't even look me in the eye.

"I know it's hard, but I wouldn't be doing my job if I let him play."

I can see her mouth start to quiver just like mine. I wait for her to build up a little steam before this next one. She'll let him have a piece of her mind. Let him have it, Mom.

She opens her mouth, and she only says one word. "Okay."

The word leaves her lips so slowly that I could snatch it from the air and hide it where no one could find it. But I can't even move.

"Mom," I say.

But I don't get any response. Okay is the only word she had left in her body. Now she's empty, and when her eyes finally look my way, she isn't behind them.

I guess Dr. McKenzie can stop me.

I slam my bedroom door and fall down on my bed. When I do, I hear a light crinkling sound beneath me.

It's the list.

I grab it and study it one more time. Tears seep out from my eyes. They pour down my cheeks and fall onto the paper, blurring some of the words and erasing the memories.

My eyes come to the first entry. *Take the Packers to the Super Bowl.* Forget what I said before. Back then, there was still a fleeting chance. Now I know the odds are zero.

As I look over the list, I finally understand what Dr. McKenzie meant when he said I could feel fine on the outside but feel bad on the inside. That's how I feel right now.

I crumple the list again and throw it in the trash. My one look-forward-to is gone.

Mom follows me through the door and sits down on the corner of my bed. Another minute goes by, and she asks me how I'm feeling.

"Bad," I say, and I wrap my pillow over my head.

"I'm sorry, dear. I know it's hard. You know I would have done something if I could."

She sits there for a long time. I know she's trying to be a good mom, but I still want her gone.

"You know, Victor," she says, but she stops. Through my pillow, I can hear the tiniest, faintest sniffle, and I can tell she wants to cry. She finally gathers her voice, and she says, "There are a lot of ways to do life."

What? What does that mean? What does that have to do with anything?

"When I say that, I mean that you never have to let anybody tell you how to live your life. Now, that may be confusing to hear, because you do need to do what the doctor tells you. But I think Dr. McKenzie was saying something else today—something other than what you heard."

I sniffle back a gob of snot. "What?"

She holds my arm and motions for me to get up. I do, and she finally looks me in the eye. "I think he was trying to tell you that you can't be you anymore," she pauses. "At least, that's what you might have taken it as. God knows I did. But my point is that you don't have to listen to anybody; not him, not even me."

"I don't have to listen to you?"

"Of course not—we both know you have that tendency anyway. But there's more to it than what it sounds like. Sometimes you do choose to listen to me. Do you know why?"

"I don't know. Cause sometimes you are right?"

"Yup. Sometimes other people know better, so they'll make rules you think are stupid, but sometimes you have to trust that they know what they're talking about."

It's hard to admit, but she's right again. I look over to her, and I can tell she's still upset with Dr. McKenzie. Maybe she's just as upset as I am. But she's still trying to stay positive.

"Okay," I say, "I get it."

"Good," she smiles and rubs my hair. "So what's it gonna be, then, mister? Are you going to live like everybody else expects you to, or are you going to live like you know you need to?"

"Like I know I need to."

"That's not good enough," she says, and now she's beaming and egging me on. "I want you to say the full sentence, like you actually believe in it!"

"Okay . . ." I hesitate, but then I finally shout, "I'm going to live like I know I need to!" The words echo off the walls. I'll bet Carl can hear them two doors over.

"Great!" Mom says. "You can put that down in writing!"

She gives me a big hug, and I manage to slide one arm around her. We hold each other for at least a minute more, trying to hold back tears again. Then, finally, she leaves me be.

I stay there a moment thinking about her words. *Put that down in writing,* she said.

Okay, I will.

I hop off my bed and grab the list out of the trash can. I unfurl its edges and flip it over to the back, slamming it on the table. With the black marker, I carefully write out *Live like I know I need to.*

I even manage a smile.

Then, I realize that there's something else that I was wrong about earlier. I do still have something to look forward to. I flip the list back over to the front, and glance down at the bottom entry.

Win the race with Tyler.

The fire in my heart is rekindled.

4

The phone rings on Thursday, and Dad hands me the cordless.

"Who is it?" I ask.

"Sean Driver." He gives a sarcastic smirk.

I take the phone and say hello. It's actually Tyler, and he's ecstatic when I tell him about Sean.

"Can I see the hat?" he says.

"I'll bring it on over," I say, but before hanging up, I add, "How was the fishing trip?"

"Oh, it sucked," he says. "Who cares?"

And that's good enough for me. I turn off the phone and quickly funnel all my sleepover stuff into my backpack. Then I swivel the famous hat onto my head. I grab my rolled-up sleeping bag from the closet, and am just about head out my door before I remember the most important part: the racer plans. I grab them and head for the door, passing by Dad on the sofa.

"Where you goin' there, buddy?" he asks as he pops a grape into his mouth.

"Over to Tyler's."

"Spending the night?"

I have my hand on the front door and turn back to face him. "No, Tyler was gonna go throw his sleeping bag off the bridge, so I thought I'd join him."

"That's my boy." He turns back to the TV and adds, "Have a good night."

Traffic is pretty slow this evening since most people are inside watching the last Packer game of the pre-season. The game's in Nashville, which is a good thing, because if it were here it would be a lot harder to get through traffic as I turn the corner onto Lombardi Avenue.

Tyler and his parents are in the living room. Without knocking, I walk in the door, and Tyler practically pounces on me.

"Can I see it?" He starts frisking my backpack and sleeping bag.

"It's on my head," I say. I take off the hat and hold it at his eye level.

"Wow," he says. He cups his hand beneath the jagged brim, and gently removes it from my hand.

"What do you think?" I say.

"It's cool."

"I told you."

"Well, let us see!" Mike hollers from the living room.

Tyler brings it over to the sofa to show his parents, but he doesn't let it out of his hand. He keeps looking at it, like he's studying an ancient hieroglyph.

I retell the story of meeting Sean, and even though I've told the story to everyone I've met over the last few days, they hang onto my words, and I love every minute of it. I even talk during the game, and they don't mind—it's just the pre-season, so the games don't count.

By the time the game is over, both Mike and Sarah are asleep on the sofa, and Tyler and I decide to go into the garage.

The air is dusty, and the single light bulb is a burnt yellow. The sheets of plywood and two-by-fours in a pile look like a beautiful altar. I turn to Tyler, and he turns to me.

"Let's get to it," I say.

There are certain specifications the car needs to obey—like size, weight, and material—so every single cut we make needs to be precise, and because we're not allowed to use the power saw (according to the International Rule Book of Tyler's Dad), it's going to take a lot more time and effort than we had thought.

"Whenever my dad makes something," I say, "he likes to get me involved a little bit. And when he makes a cut with a saw, he always says, 'measure twice, cut once.' It's a thing you're supposed to do just to make sure it's all accurate."

"Measure twice, cut once?"

"Yeah."

"How could you make a cut more than once? That doesn't even make sense," he smirks.

"Hey, let's not start this sassy stuff already," I say. I giggle and give him a little punch below the shoulder.

"Hey, that hurts!"

"Oh, I barely nicked you."

"Yeah, but I got this big bruise from fishing." He lifts up his sleeve and rubs a splotch of dark yellow skin covering most of his upper arm.

"Sick!" I say. "How'd you get a bruise from fishing? Did a salmon yank you overboard?" I regret saying that right away, though, cause that probably is what happened—or something close to it—cause Tyler's such a small guy.

"Only joking," I say.

Tyler shakes it off. "It doesn't even matter. Can we get started now?"

I finally give in and help him prop a board on top of a pair of sawhorses. We measure out (twice) and draw a line with a pencil down the middle. I take the saw in hand and line it up perfectly. Finally, our work has begun.

"So how was the fishing trip, then?" I say. "I know you said it stunk, but what kind of stink?"

Tyler just shrugs.

"C'mon, we gotta have something to talk about while we work- on- this-" I say as I grind away the last remaining splinters that connected the two boards. Tyler catches the falling end, and I catch the other.

"Well," he says, "it was kind of like the time you went with us. My uncles yell a lot, and so does my dad when he's with them and they're all drinking. They act nice around my mom and everything, but they get angry really easily."

I realize how lucky I am when I think about my parents. They'll have a glass of wine every now and then, but I've never seen them drunk. When you live in a state that named its baseball team after beer, you get a lot of kids just like Tyler who grow up surrounded by it. I hate to think that Tyler's uncles used to be just like him when they were little; that would mean that Tyler's on the exact same path.

"Do you ever tell them you're having a lousy time?" I say. "Maybe it would be nice to show them how you feel."

"I don't think they would even care."

"How about your mom? I don't think she would make you go on those trips anymore if she knew how you were being treated."

"No, Vic. They're family, and they're good people. Telling on them wouldn't help; it would just screw up the family."

I want to help him, but if I try to, he'll just say I don't know what it's like. Then again, I guess I really don't know what it's like.

"Tyler, I'm sorry."

"Don't be. I'm feeling fine."

"No, not that. I mean I'm sorry about thinking I know everything. You're a smart guy. You can figure it out."

"Thanks."

"But Tyler?"

"Yeah?"

"That still doesn't mean you shouldn't listen to the things people have to tell you." I wait a moment. I think back to Mom, and I try my best to remember her words.

"You know something I learned pretty recently?" I say.

"Hm?" He grunts, finally looking over.

"It has to do with my sickness," I say, and Tyler quickly turns his eyes to a spot on the floor. I continue, "And I know you don't like to talk about it, but it's real Tyler. It really is."

"I know it is."

"I know you know—that's not the point. I learned that you need to live your own way, but still listen to other people, cause sometimes they know what's best."

"I know that," he says.

"Good. It's hard to be brave when everyone's bigger than you, and I know as well as anybody it's hard to be brave when you don't think you can win. But there's something great about bravery."

Tyler is like a sculpture, not moving an inch.

I lean down next to him and say, "Bravery is unbeatable."

Tyler keeps staring at the floor.

"Look," I say, "you're a small guy, right? But being brave doesn't have anything to do with how big you are. It has to do with how you react to the things that scare you."

Tyler looks at the wall, and this time he speaks. "That's all good stuff, Vic . . . but I'm still too small. That's a fact. It can't be changed. So if I say anything to my uncles, well . . . I just can't win."

I don't know what to say to that. What can I say if he won't listen?

I look down at the board in my hands. It's perfectly cut. It's beautiful. I go over to the corner of the garage and pick up the blueprints to study them. With a soapbox racer, everything has to fit perfectly in order for the car to work. But even with all of the regulations, there's one X factor that makes a huge difference. I turn to Tyler.

"Being small has its advantages," I say.

"Name one."

"The soapbox racer," I say. I show him the plans. "The rules say that the car can't weigh more than 200 pounds. But that's with the driver included. That means the lighter you are, the more weight we can add to the right spots of the car."

Tyler finally turns around to look at me. "You mean . . . I'm going to be the driver?"

"You have no choice," I say with a nasty smile. "You're the lightest of us two. You give us the best chance to win."

Tyler can't even say a word. I knew from the start he wouldn't want to drive, and that's why I waited until we had begun building to tell him. I walk over to his side and hold out the plans. "Sooner or later, you're going to have to step out of your comfort zone," I say.

Tyler studies the plans for a moment, and a fold forms in his eyebrow.

"Look at this," he finally says. "The plans don't even have a chair for the driver to sit in. Am I supposed to just scrape my butt against the cement or something?"

That was a bit harsher than I was expecting. I take the plans out of his hands and study them. Before I can say anything, he says, "If I'm driving this thing, my comfort zone won't be anywhere near it." He starts to chuckle, and I manage to eke out a small grin.

"So, you really think I can do it?" he says.

"Yeah. I think you can."

The crickets are chirping as one o'clock in the morning rounds the corner. Our sleeping bags are sprawled out across the living room floor. I lie looking at the ceiling and think about how the end of summer is fast approaching. It's a bummer, sure, but I'm glad that this is how we get to end it.

I get a rude awakening around seven. It's Dad. For some reason, he steps through the hallway and into the living room with Tyler's parents.

"There you are, Victor," he says.

"Wasgonon?" I rub my eyes.

"You forget to do something yesterday when you left the house?"

"Wha—? No."

"You sure?" He spots my backpack on the couch and starts digging through the pockets.

"What are you doing?" I say. Now I'm fully awake.

Dad stops shuffling his hand for a moment, and then I see him pull out the cordless phone.

"Oh."

"Yeah."

"I'm sorry."

He reaches his hand down in front of me. "Well, c'mon now. I might as well take you home while I'm over here."

Tyler is just now stirring in his sleeping bag. I let out a huge yawn and get up right away. I learned to listen to what Dad says when I know he's angry, cause it usually just causes more problems if I don't.

Dad throws my bike in the trunk of his car, then we both hop in and slam the doors. But he doesn't start the car.

"I'm sorry about the phone," I say, my head pointed straight at the floor mat, "but you didn't have to come over just for a dumb phone. You have your cell phone."

"Victor, it's not just about the phone," he says. "We really need you to start being more responsible around the house. You know your mother has been working herself hard to try and find a job so we don't end up stuck in that little apartment forever. And she needs to be around the phone in case someone gives her a call."

I sink my head lower. "I didn't realize that."

Dad sighs. "Well, it's true."

"I'm really sorry."

"I know you are. I just need you to stop having to be sorry."

"What?"

"I mean you've gotta think, Victor. You've gotta start thinking about others a little more. I've noticed it a lot lately."

"I think about others!" I yell. I didn't mean to say that too angrily. Now that it's out, I actually start to feel it.

"You think about others, I know. But Vic, there's more to it than that. Like the other day; Mom told you to be home before it got dark."

I groan. "I already told you guys. I was one minute late. I even told Jared and Randy."

"I know, I know, Victor. I know that you just wanted to play with your friends, and I know you weren't trying to hurt anybody, but this is what I'm talking about. You still weren't thinking about your mom. She gave you that strict rule to be home."

"It was a bogus rule."

"That doesn't matter, Victor."

"Yes it does! Why should I bother following a rule if I think it's stupid?"

"You just proved my point about your 'me' attitude! You weren't thinking about Mom at all, only about how stupid you thought her rule was."

"Well—"

"Vic, when you really care about someone, you set yourself aside to make them happy. You need to learn that."

Then, I remember what Mom said to me. *They'll go off making rules you think are stupid, but sometimes you have to trust that they know what they're talking about, even when it doesn't make sense to you.*

"I got it," I say.

"I don't think you do."

"I got it!" I yell, swinging my head around to meet his eyes.

We park in the lot outside our apartment. Dad kills the engine, and I'm first to head inside, leaving my bike in the trunk. Mom is waiting at the table with a mug of coffee. She says hi, and I say hi back and let her know that I'm sorry. She seems a little bit less agitated than Dad was. I give her a hug and go to my bed.

A minute later I hear Dad pry his way through the squeaky front screen door. He tramples to the kitchen in his heavy boots that send vibrations through the floorboards and up into my mattress. I lie on my side with my eyes wide open, just listening to everything on the other side of that wall. The phone clangs down onto the receiver in the kitchen, and I hear a short beep. "Two messages," Dad says to Mom. The phone beeps again and on comes the first one. It's a man, probably Dad's age. I get up and head over to the door to hear a little better.

"Hello, I'm calling looking for Carrie Ross. This is Bradley Stephens, one of the managers here at Stephens Electric."

I immediately feel a tear rush to the corner of my eye. Maybe I did cost mom a job. Just because I couldn't remember to hang up the stupid phone. I creak open the door just enough to slip out without making a sound. The message continues playing.

"I'm calling to let you know that we have received your application and résumé. It looks quite impressive, so I was hoping to set up an initial interview to get to know you a little better. Hope that would be alright. I've got a few other applicants I'll be calling here shortly, so please let me know as soon as possible if we'll be able to set up an appointment. Thanks a lot. Goodbye."

I gulp and tiptoe down the hall into the entryway to the kitchen. The dial tone beeps again, as if it's angry at me.

Then I see something wonderful. My parents are hugging. They're actually happy. I let the wall behind me catch my body. They notice me in the corner, and then they beckon me over with their hands.

"I'm sorry, Mom."

"It's okay, Victor. It's okay. Everything's okay now."

Before I even reach them, the phone beeps again and the next message comes on; another middle-aged man. I suppose it's another employer calling for Mom. I'm even hopeful, if that's not taking the first one for granted.

But not one of us is expecting what comes next.

"Hello, Mr. and Mrs. Ross. My name is Henry Summit, and I'm calling on behalf of the Dream Foundation. As you may know, the Dream Foundation raises money to help children with illnesses to reach their dreams. We've received word through a string of sources about your child Victor's condition, and though we have not received an official application from you, it is my understanding that we are willing to make an exception based on . . . personal referral. It is the foundation's hope that by granting Victor his dream, we will be able help in heightening his self-confidence and endurance as he goes through this hard time. So with that said, we would like to officially offer you our full service. Pending your acceptance of the offer, we would need either one of you to come with Victor down to our office sometime in the coming weeks in order to confirm your participation. Until then, a simple returning of this call is all we need to hold your place. On behalf of the foundation, I wish you and your entire family all the best. Goodbye."

The machine clicks, and then declares, "End of new messages."

I look at Dad, then look at Mom. I might as well look in the mirror because we all have the same blank face.

"Was that real?" I say.

Neither Mom nor Dad say anything. They look like they want to but can't seem to do it.

"Thank you," I say. I take them into a hug, but Dad shuffles himself out of my grip.

"Victor?"

"Yeah?"

"Are you saying you had nothing to do with this?"

I step back. "What do you mean?"

"You didn't do anything?" Mom says.

"Of course not. Why?"

Dad looks at me, curious. "Because," he says, "neither did we."

"What?"

I take another step back. Both of their faces are straight.

"We had no idea," Mom says.

"Well, then who told them?" I say.

Dad smiles. "Victor, it doesn't matter who told them. It matters that it's happening."

I suppose he's right, but no matter how much I feel like jumping and celebrating and smiling, I can't stop wondering.

Wait . . . smiling . . .

The sparkle from their smiling teeth instantly snaps me back to last Monday, to a different smile that I saw. It was the best smile in the world. And then I remember the conversation.

It was Sean Driver. That's why he wanted my full name. He was trying to find me, and he succeeded. I can't help but mimic the best smile in the world.

Then Dad butts in. "So?"

My thoughts fizzle. "What?" I say.

"It's the Dream Foundation, Victor. What's your dream?"

And I remember the last thing Sean and I said to each other that day.

"I'll see you later, Sean!"
"I'm sure you will."

I realize that there's really no choice to be made.

"I'm going to a football game," I say.

We hug one more time, and I thank God for bringing Sean into my life.

TIMEOUT

Fourteen Years Earlier

Before there was Sean Driver, there was Elijah White, a defensive lineman. Elijah singlehandedly set the benchmark for fear in football. If you lined up against him, you knew you were punching a one-way ticket straight into the dirt. Elijah was that kind of man. He was a competitor, as fierce as they come. But as much passion as he had for football, he had more passion for his faith. He even gained the nickname "The Minister."

He shocked the sports world when he announced that he would not return to Philadelphia for a ninth season. Instead, he would head north to the small city of Green Bay to join the Packers.

"I feel that I have been led here by God," Elijah announced. "He has brought me here for a reason."

What Elijah didn't say was that there was a second reason he made the move, a reason almost as important as God. That reason was Gordon Fisher. Elijah saw in Gordon the same drive for success that he had himself. And there was no denying the connection. As soon as Elijah put on his Packers uniform, he became a spiritual mentor to Gordon and to the team as a whole.

Not only that, but Elijah provided the last ingredient for success that the team needed—a defensive powerhouse. With Gordon on offense, and

Elijah on defense, the Packers were primed and ready to be the most dominant team in the league.

2ND QUARTER:
DREAMS DO COME CLOSE

5

Normally on the first day of school, there's a stack of breakfast food spread across the kitchen table. Mom does that. But this morning she's just as busy as me. It's her interview day—kind of like her own first day. Hopefully there will be a real one in the future. It's "quite the conundrum," she says, getting ready for an electrician interview. She has to look nice, but can't look *too* nice or it'll look like she can't fit in at a blue-collar job, and she says it's especially difficult for a woman to pull that off. She walks out of the hallway bathroom in a black shirt with dark denim jeans and jacket.

"Looking good," Dad says, and he kisses her. In the meantime, I've slipped my backpack over one shoulder of my new short-sleeve polo shirt. I'm ready for takeoff.

Dad turns to me. "Not looking too bad yourself, kiddo." My parents both look at me the same way they did the morning of the perfect day. It's been two days since the perfect day, but the perfection still hasn't worn off.

Dad called the people from the Dream Foundation, and the offer was confirmed. That was the best part to me. Hearing that it really wasn't some kind of stupid prank. We're headed down to the office in a few days to sign some papers and let them know what my "dream" will be.

I give Dad a high five and Mom a kiss on the cheek before I blast out the door. Immediately, I feel alone. Normally on the first day of school there would also be a buddy walking the sidewalk with me. I wonder if Tyler feels the same way I do.

The morning playground is alive with students giggling and running all around. Me, though, I'm just sitting here coolly on the monkey bars, one leg hunched up and the other dangling over the edge, waiting for fifth grade to begin. Jared and Randy are next to me, and I've just dropped the big bomb on them— I won't be playing football this season.

"That's . . . that's a load of crap!" Jared scowls.

"Your doctor's a jerk! He can't do that to us!" Randy says.

"Us?" I say.

"The team!" he says. "We need you this year!"

"I don't know—"

"Yes, we do. That's unfair, Vic. There's gotta be something we can do."

"There's nothing. I already tried."

I huff a big sigh, and sit there for a minute in silence, disappointed in myself even though I know I shouldn't be. But finally Jared gives me a break from it all.

"So, have you decided which Packer game you're going to?" he says.

"You should go to the one against the Vikings, week ten," Randy says. "That's bound to be a really big game."

"No, he can't," Jared says. "It's too big a risk going that long from now."

"Shut the hell up, Jared. He's not gonna die tomorrow."

"I'm saying there's a chance he *might*. You agree with me, don't you, Vic?"

Telling them to stop won't do any real help, so I guess I'll just have to toughen up and play along.

"Actually I was planning on surviving at least until Christmas," I say. "That way I can see all the cool toys I'll never get to play with." I give a little chuckle and they laugh along, but I feel hollow in my stomach afterward.

Along the blacktop, I see a pack of third graders walking toward the basketball courts. I see Tyler trailing along the back, not really paying attention to anyone or being paid attention to. Then he spots me. He smiles wide, and waves with his whole arm. I start to give a little hand wave back, and then Jared notices, and I put my hand down.

"Did that kid finally make it out of kindergarten?" he jokes.

"Shut up," I say, and I push him off balance.

"Hey!" he says, grabbing onto a monkey bar. "He's small, that's all I was saying."

"And a little bit weird," Randy adds.

"Yeah, and a little bit weird."

I don't say anything else about him. I just change the subject back to the Packers. "I'm thinking about going to the game against the Bears, week five," I say.

"Perfect," Jared says. "But you'd better ask if you can bring another person, cause I'm going with you."

I smile. "Nice try," I say, and I give him another shove.

The bell finally rings, and we start climbing down the ladder. As I pick up my backpack off the ground, I say to them both, "I'll see what I can do."

Ms. Sherman meets us in the doorway of our new classroom.

"Welcome back to school, everyone," she says with a soft, sweet voice. She is younger than most teachers I've seen. She has a nice smile, too. Not like the grumps I've had in the past. She walks around the room with a chart with our names and pictures on it.

"I made you all nametags so you can get to know each other better. On the bottom, I want you to fill out your favorite hobby. Then we'll go around the room and share."

When she comes to me, she smiles, and says, "You must be Victor," and she hands me my nametag. Her smile is bright, and it warms me up—even more than Sean Driver's. Maybe this class will be okay.

I just twiddle the nametag in my hand, and don't even remember to write anything down.

After the day gets out, I book it home to see if there's anything new to report. I get about halfway there when I realize that I didn't even stop to meet Tyler. I figure he won't mind. He's probably home by now anyway.

I ride up to the patchy front lawn and throw my bike into the grass. I pry open the screen door and step inside. There aren't any lights on, but I hear some movement in the kitchen, so I head on in.

"Mom?"

"Hey, Victor." I step into the kitchen and see her seated at the table.

"Any news today?"

"No, nobody's called."

"Oh . . . okay." I'm just about to leave to drop off my backpack in my room, but then I notice that she doesn't look so good.

"How—how did the interview go?"

"Oh, not so well." She turns her face. It casts a shadow over the sun coming in through the windows, but she quickly flickers it into a smile. "Don't worry. It'll be okay. Work will come."

"Okay . . . are you sure you're okay?"

"Yeah. A little frustrated. But it'll be okay. That's what I keep telling myself, cause I know it will."

"How do you know?" Then I drop my backpack right there on the floor, and go take a seat across from her at the table.

"Well, we've got a pretty good life. I mean, look around you." I do what she says. The kitchen is small and cramped, and there's stuff eating away at the cabinets. I turn back and give her a puzzled look, and she continues, "There are a *lot* of worse places to stay in the world, Victor. You just don't know it because this is the worst one we've had. But trust me, even if I never get a job again, even if we never make it out of this apartment, we'll be okay."

"Okay," I say. I sit there a little while longer, just taking in all the crappiness in our home and trying to figure out if it really is so crappy.

That Sunday is opening day for the Packers. They're playing against the Eagles, who are heavily favored and many say will make it to the Super Bowl. I like to be an optimist, so I'll say we have a chance.

We're all planning on heading over to Tyler's house to watch with his family. It'll be the first time I've been with Tyler since the beginning of school, but the week went by so fast that it hasn't really seemed that long at all. I doubt he's even noticed.

Street traffic is too heavy on game day, so we have to walk. Dad packs a potato salad and green bean casserole in a small cooler that he plans on hauling with us.

But as we get ready to leave, I get a call from Randy.

"What's up?" I say.

"Packer party at my house. We've got tons of food. Jared's coming over too. You wanna come?"

"I can't. My family's going to Tyler's house."

"Oh." Randy goes silent.

"Hold on a minute," I say. I pull the phone away and turn to Mom. She's fixing her favorite Packer earrings in the hallway mirror. "Mom," I say, "can I go to Randy's instead? His family's having a big party."

She turns to me. "You can if you really want to. Could Tyler go too?"

I'm about to ask Randy, but I pull the phone away again. "I don't know if he'd get along with these guys," I say.

"Oh, well if you think you'd have more fun, then you're welcome to go."

I put the phone to my ear one more time. I tell Randy, "I'll be there in a few minutes."

I weave my bike through the herd of foam Cheeseheads on my way down Oneida Street. I nearly collide with a family that decided it would be fun to tailgate in the middle of the sidewalk.

A lot of people are wearing Gordon Fisher's jersey. It's no secret that it might be his last year playing, so people are getting all the mileage they can out of their threads.

I make my way across Lombardi Avenue and over to Randy's house a few blocks away. The front door is wide open, and there are lots of people chatting, drinking, and playing corn hole on the front lawn. I shimmy by a few people crowding the front hallway, and I find Randy and Jared in the living room sitting in front of the big screen. I squeeze in next to them, and we get ready for kickoff. The crowd roars, but I can hear it more from the stadium outside than I can from the TV.

Packers quarterback Gordon Fisher takes a labored breath near the 40-yard line of the south end of Lambeau Field. The air is still warm, but a hint of the fall to come seeps into his lungs.

We can do this, he thinks.

He scans the field to ensure that his teammates are ready, and in doing so, he takes in the position of every Eagles defender. Eleven of them. Eleven Eagles separate him and his men from the promised land. He calls out the cadence without even needing to think. "Green Nineteen! Green Nineteen!" The words have become a part of his being. "Set hut!"

In an instant, the round piece of leather is shoved into his hands. It's so precious that he barely feels worthy to touch it, but he accepts it graciously and steps back to see the land that lies before him. Only forty yards to go on this lush, green field. As he examines it all, the green grass withers away, and he and his men are left wandering in the desert waiting for the scavengers to pick them clean.

Immediately the Eagles begin to attack, their sharp claws piercing the sides of the men that are trying to protect him. Gordon knows that he needs to think quickly, but the brilliant sun from the south flares directly into his eyes, confusing his sense of direction.

A claw reaches for his right shoulder and tears his arm backward, but Gordon protects the leather by bringing it in close to his side. Ahead he sees a large man clothed in green, an ally, being attacked by two other Eagles. But the man swats at his enemies to keep them away. With that one last glimmer of freedom, Gordon heaves the ball to his teammate, and as it leaves his fingertips, he looks ahead to see the scene before him. The desert is completely dry, and there's no chance for rain. The team that he once believed in is in a deep, emaciated despair. The promised land is gone, and he is immediately engulfed in a frenzy of Eagles.

"Interception!"

The words of the announcer on TV barely make it through the desperate groans that fill the living room, which are closely followed by mumbles of "should've retired" and "not the same anymore." It's Gordon's second big mistake of the day after an earlier fumble, and both of those mistakes have stranded us in a 13-13 tie.

With less than one minute to go, Gordon is losing faith. Now, he can only sit back and watch as his punter boots the ball away to the opposing team. His stomach rumbles in a way that makes him feel like he's going to be sick. As the ball flies through the arid sky, Gordon watches his last opportunity at glory float away in its wake.

We had another chance. We should have scored.

The somber mood of the thousands of fans is enough to rip the last thread of hope from his heart. But suddenly, he feels a rumble, and it isn't coming from his stomach. An earthquake. That has to be it. But there are no earthquakes in Wisconsin. But what else could make the earth shake with such a force?

He watches the ball strike the helmet of the opposing receiver and tumble back into the hands of his own teammate. The crowd roars in ecstasy, jumping up and down in celebration. The force of the feet hitting the bleachers in unison is enough to send a seismic wave through the stadium.

The field goal team rushes onto the field, and the rookie kicker boots the ball through the goalposts with no time left and puts the Packers in the lead. It's all over in one swift motion. Gordon collapses to his knees in relief and only has one thought pass through his mind.

God must be a Packer fan.

The living room explodes, everyone hugging each other and swinging each other around, and I'm pretty sure I knocked a bowl of chip dip off the coffee table, but none of that matters now. I dance around the living room and hug people that I don't even know. Everyone in the room shares a single heartbeat, and all I can think is that God must be Packer fan.

Only weeks later, our team is the biggest buzz around the league. In fact, they're one of the only teams left with a perfect record of 4-0.

The team is one of many reasons I'm flashing a big smile these days. Dad and I went to the Dream Foundation office and confirmed that I will be going to the game this weekend against the Bears.

But for me, it's not as much about the gift itself. It's the fact that someone cared enough to make this happen for me. That, and the fact that I get to share the fun with someone else.

When we leave the foundation office that afternoon, Dad asks me who I want to take to the game. I explain how Jared said I should ask for another ticket, and how it made me realize that there was someone who really deserved it. I'm not sure I want to see Jared's face when he discovers that it isn't him.

When we get home, I sift through the stack of papers in the corner of my room and find the blueprints for the soapbox derby racer. They haven't been touched in weeks. I go grab the phone out of the kitchen, and dial. Tyler answers on the other end.

"Hey buddy," I say. "It's been awhile."

6

My eyes pop open. I rub my chilly feet together a few times to create some friction, then I tuck the end of the covers back under my legs to trap in the heat. Steam is rising from the ground outside my window, and I'm guessing there's a thin coat of frost on the grass. It's early October, but it takes me a moment to remember exactly which day. This is the day that dreams are made of.

On my floor are my clothes for the day: black tennis shoes, a pair of yellow athletic shorts, one jersey with *DRIVER* on the back in all capitals, and one chopped-up-and-autographed Packers hat. I laid them out last night so I wouldn't miss a beat.

After dressing, I walk out into the hall and toward the kitchen. Dad meets me halfway down the hall. He's carrying a mug of coffee and a thin roll of newspaper. He notices my clothes and he says, "Coach called wondering where his star receiver was. I told him he couldn't play today cause the quilt monster in his room wasn't letting him out of bed." He smiles and smacks the jagged brim of my hat down over my face with the newspaper.

I follow my nose through the living room and into the kitchen—the source of an amazing smell. Mom turns from the stove and leans over the counter. "Hey there, bud. Take a seat and let me know how cool your mom is."

I lift up my hat and my eyes go wide. The table in front of me has a feast. One plate has hash browns and toast with bacon and sausage on the side. One plate has pancakes that are shaped like the Packer's G logo, and the eggs are sunny-side up with the whites dyed green. A glass of milk is poured into the faded plastic Packer cup that came with a meal from

McDonald's a long time ago. It's all so beautiful—at least, before I sit down and start scarfing.

I'll have to wait a while before the game, because it's the prime time game this week. But that also means that it will be broadcast coast-to-coast. Dad joked with me the other day that I'll for sure make it on national television—when they show the aerial view of the entire stadium from the blimp.

Prime time is only one of the reasons I chose this game in the first place. The other is the opponent. The Packer-Bear game goes back almost a hundred years. It's a rivalry that has torn families apart, it's so vicious. The Bears made it to the Super Bowl last season, but they've lost a lot of good players since then, and they've only won one game so far this year. After doing the math, I figured Tyler and I should be in for a treat.

Some dark clouds roll off the bay late in the evening. Slowly, the neighborhood becomes spotted with lights from kitchen windows. Pots and pans are clanking together, preparing all sorts of delicious and fattening tailgate food.

Because we live so close to the stadium, I've grown up surrounded by this certain culture that most people won't experience in their lives. First, on game days, everybody's lawn becomes a parking lot. Depending on how close you are to the field, some people make $20 or $30 for each car they let park on their property.

The next tradition is the art of front-yard tailgating. People literally bring their living room furniture out on their grass, and surround it with a high definition TV and a charcoal grill. Sure, tonight will be a little bit colder than normal, but that just means they've got to cozy up closer to the ones they love.

I stare out into the street from my living room couch and watch all the commotion unfold. Every set of headlights on this street is pointed toward the stadium. But then a pair of lights peels slowly up my side of the street and pull into my apartment's driveway. The lights belong to a black car so long it can barely fit its back end in from the road. I turn and yell, "Mom! Dad! They brought a limo!"

I'm out on the lawn before I end the sentence. My parents aren't far behind, and I almost slam the screen door in their faces. I get to the side of the car, and examine all its tinted black windows.

The front door opens, and the driver graciously exits and tips his hat. "Victor Ross?" I nod and tip my hat back. "Pleased to meet you. My name is Charles, and I'll be your chauffer this evening on behalf of the Dream Foundation. Ah, and you are his parents."

Dad looks a little bit skeptical as he shakes his hand. "Hey, we really appreciate this special treatment and all," he says, "but was it really necessary to pick him up in a car that's longer than the distance it'll be travelling?"

"You cannot put a price on the smile of a child," Charles says, and he manages a smirk, as if he also thinks its bit much.

I stare more closely into the windows, which reflect all the lights of the night.

"How's this feel?" Mom asks. "Pretty cool, huh?"

"Yeah!" I say.

"You all ready to go then, Champ?" Dad asks.

"Ready," I nod.

"You have everything?"

"Yep."

"Wallet? Money?"

"Yes."

"Camera?"

"Ummm . . ." I pat myself down, then look up. "Short on cameras."

Mom sighs and says, "I'll be right back," and she runs into the apartment. Dad takes the time to ask me if I forgot to bring the cordless phone with me, too, and I give him a light punch in the arm.

Mom is back in an instant. "Here you go," she says. She hands me the camera and tousles my hair. She hugs me, telling me how special I am and how proud of me she is.

Dad gives me a hug and then a pat on the back. "Take 'em all the way," he says.

"What do you mean?"

"The Super Bowl. You'll take 'em there."

I give an awkward smile and wave goodbye. Charles takes me to the limo, opens the back door, and I take a step into luxury. Black leather seating and wooden trim decorate the interior. There's a mirror that stretches the entire length of the ceiling, making it look like gravity was flipped upside down.

Then I see Tyler. It's the first time in weeks, which makes me feel both happy and guilty at the same time. I look around. In here, we're protected by the tinted windows. Nobody can see that I'm with him, and nobody can judge me for it. But I wish I didn't ever need the tinted windows. Tyler is a real friend, and I haven't treated him that way at all.

As soon as I get a good look at Tyler, I can't help it and I burst out laughing. Tyler is dressed in the most ridiculous Packers gear I've ever seen, and I can only imagine that he made it all himself. He nods to me, and tilts his Cheesehead made out of paper-mache. "Hello, Vic," he says.

Before I can even respond, the window divider slides down. "We all set back there?" Charles says through the opening. Tyler and I both nod. "Good, so we're off to the game!"

The engine roars to a start, and we begin pulling out of the driveway. When I look out the window, I see Mom and Dad waving vigorously at an empty spot in the limo, apparently hoping through the tinted windows that they'd hit their mark.

I turn back to Tyler. Up close, I notice that he looks a little scraggly.

"So . . . what's been up?" I say. That's when I realize something. Not only have I not talked to Tyler in a while, it's been so long since I've *seen* Tyler that I feel awkward just talking to him, like we were guests at a birthday party, forced to meet each other. I can't even think of any topic.

"How's the soapbox racer looking these days?" I say.

Then I regret my question. Tyler shrugs. "It's about the same, only now it's over in the corner."

"Oh."

The air between us feels empty.

"Tyler," I say, "there's something I've been wanting to bring up. Well, I feel like I could've been a better friend to you lately."

Tyler stirs in his seat. "What do you mean?"

"Well . . . I haven't even really talked to you since we started school."

"Oh. Yeah, well, that's okay."

"Well, I just wanted to let you know it doesn't *feel* okay."

"You've got a lot of stuff you're doing lately."

"But I don't really. I mean, yeah, there's a lot of stuff going on with me being sick and all, but really, I mean, none of that matters."

"It's okay, Vic," he says. Then he looks down on the floor, like he's a dog that's done something bad. But I don't want Tyler to be a dog. I want him to be my friend. Most of all, I want to earn back his friendship. But I'm not sure how I can.

The limo pulls up to the plaza outside the front of the stadium, and the engine purrs slowly to a halt. We hear Charles open his door, then ours. He peers inside and says, "Welcome to Lambeau Field," as though it's my first time here. Tyler and I step out the door from luxury into something far more heavenly. The lights, the atmosphere, the brilliant shine of the plate glass entry. I know instantly that I'm wrong—I've never really been to this stadium.

In the plaza, there are two statues; one of Curly Lambeau, the Packer's founder, and one of Vince Lombardi, considered the best football coach ever, who won five championships in only nine seasons with the team. I always see them perched on their pedestals when I ride my bike past, but now I recognize how they're standing. Tyler and I walk up to Curly. He's dressed down in a sweatshirt and sweatpants, as if he just got done on the practice field back in 1920. His one hand is clutching a fat football, and the other one is stretched out and pointing straight at Lombardi. It's like he's pointing to the future, and the football is something that only true champions can hold. It's like he's saying, "Go long, Vince. I'll hit you deep."

"Welcome!" A voice tears me from my fantasy. Charles introduces a man wearing a dark blue sports coat—the representative from the foundation.

"I'm Victor," I say and shake his hand.

"Hello, Victor. You can call me Hank," he says. "Well, it looks like you got here alright. How was the limo ride?"

"It was great," I say plainly.

"It was short," Tyler says.

Hank leans down next to him. "You make that sound like a bad thing," he says. "Not all of the great things in life will last a long time, but that doesn't mean you can't enjoy them. It makes you appreciate the short time even more." Then he flashes me a smile, and it takes me a moment to realize that he's not talking about the limo ride.

We part ways with Charles for now, and Hank beckons us to follow him into the atrium.

As we're crossing the plaza, Tyler says, "Plus, we still have the limo ride back." Hank looks forward and tries to hide a grin.

When we get inside, Hank hands us two tickets—seats at midfield—two gift shop vouchers for $100 each and two concessions vouchers for $50 each.

"Now," he says, "we're going to meet back here when the game's over, which should be around—"

"Wait, you're not coming with us?" I ask, maybe sounding a bit more hopeful than I had intended.

Hank only smiles and closes his briefcase, saying, "It was my understanding that your dream did not involve being babysat by an old stranger." I manage a chuckle. I don't think he's that old.

"Any other questions?" We both shake our heads no. "Great," he says. "Now just make sure to have an absolutely great time!" He pats us both on the head and walks away, just like that.

Only then do I realize how many people are pouring through the atrium. The bobbing heads are like a river of green and yellow waiting to spill into the stadium bowl. Tyler yells to me over the sound of the rapids that he wants to get some stuff at the shop before the game begins. I grab his hand, and we both paddle hard upstream.

The shop is packed to the doors and we'd be hard pressed, literally, to try to fit between the aisles.

"Let's try upstairs," Tyler tugs my shoulder, and I follow his lead up the staircase. Once we reach the landing, I stop to take a breather. I lean against the railing and look up.

The light in the ceiling is nothing out of the ordinary, but something about it flickers in my memory. I turn to look outside through the large plate-glass windows onto the corner where Oneida Street meets Lombardi Avenue. Now it's flowing with pedestrians, but it was practically deserted just over a month ago, the night I stood there with my bike looking at the very same light that's above my head now. It makes me remember Mom and her work on the stadium. That light is ours. All of these lights are ours. I feel a sudden surge of comfort, like she's here with me.

Tyler heads down the main aisle and beckons me to follow. Suddenly I remember where I am and why I'm here. I follow his lead. "I'm coming," I say. "Let's get some stuff and get into the stadium. The game is about to start."

Gordon Fisher opens his eyes, but the darkness is so thick around him that he can't even tell the difference. It swallows his other senses, and soon it seems as though nothing exists other than his mind and the hope that there's a way out.

"Hello?" the word leaves his lips and slices through the air. He extends his left hand, and though he can't see a thing, he feels pine needles prick into his fingers.

I'm in a forest, he thinks.

A twig snaps somewhere in front of him, but he still can't see. He feels his way around the tree, but quickly finds that the branches of the others are far too thick to let him through.

He steps back and calls to the world, "Is there anybody out there?"

The response is a growl that shakes the ground beneath him. Gordon turns. The sound came from somewhere off to his right. It sounded like a Bear, and it was close enough to make Gordon's legs start to tremble.

Another twig snaps, this time off to his left, and Gordon dreads the fact that the first beast is not alone. He frantically begins searching for a clearing in the trees, but they're so dense that they might as well be a wall.

Gordon hears the Bears move closer and closer. A third makes its presence known, and as they step even closer, they seem to multiply.

Desperate for any outlet, Gordon swipes his hands to feel what he cannot see. Two, three, four times, he swings his arms, but he can't even think of what he'd possibly hope to find.

Then something clanks to the ground. Gordon holds his hand in pain, but quickly shakes it off. The sound that it made is completely foreign, which means the object, whatever it is, couldn't possibly be natural to the forest.

Gordon bends down and feels for the object, unsure if it might somehow work to his advantage. His hands caress the dry, fallen pine needles as he sweeps them across the ground. Another growl from the bears remind him that his time is quickly dwindling.

His left hand falls on a smooth pipe. He notices for the first time that a light reflects off its surface, but he cannot tell from where the light took its origin. All he knows is that the pipe is not a pipe at all. It's a shotgun.

He takes the shotgun.

He climbs to his feet, and without thinking, he takes off running. The trees that had circled him begin to part, creating a pathway in the exact direction that he's running. It's then that Gordon realizes that the trees were on his team. The wall that they had formed was meant to protect him from danger for as long as possible.

"Keep it up, guys! Just a little bit longer!"

A Bear leaps onto the path only a few feet behind him. Its hairy, dark figure stands out even against the pitch-black background. The earth shakes as it stands to his hind feet and lets out a terrifying roar.

He sprints, but the Bear sprints after him and soon every beast in the entire forest is chasing him. With each step, he feels the pads of their enormous feet causing the ground to crumble. The trees around him begin to wither, and soon their branches are no match for the thundering claws; they simply snap in a pathetic attempt to slow them down.

With the trees no longer on his side, Gordon realizes that he is alone, and he is no longer in a forest. He's in a dry, endless field.

By the glint of his gun, he turns back to see the dark figures closing in. With not even a prayer at his disposal, he turns around and blindly aims the barrel at the biggest, meanest Bear, and he pulls the trigger.

The bullets do not scatter—they spiral around each other, then they join together to form a single, large bullet. The bullet collides with its mark, but it does not go through; it gets absorbed by the meanest, biggest Bear.

The last thing Gordon sees before closing his eyes are the two malicious eyes of the Bear, staring straight into his soul. They only laugh as Gordon falls helplessly to the ground. For the first time, he is defeated.

A hateful curse word rings behind my right ear. Then, like echoes across a quarry, the others begin to follow.

I throw both hands in front of my face to try to shield my eyes from the scene, but my fingers are caught by the jagged brim of my hat, and it frays them apart. Through the gap in my fingers, I see the Bears' defensive line now blocking as if they were on offense. They make a little pocket around their teammate, who snagged the ball effortlessly out of the air as though he controlled the wind. He carries the ball snugly in his arm and a Packers receiver tries to latch on and bring him down. The Bear dodges and sprints a few more yards downfield before finally stumbling to the ground.

There's a pit it my stomach that swallows all the happiness and carries it to another dimension. I keep my hands in front of my face. Through the gap in my left hand, I see Gordon sitting on the ground with legs spread and hands fallen limp in between. Something is different. Usually when Gordon throws an interception, he'll be the first one to charge the defender and try to redeem himself. But not this time. This time, he looks like a child in a sandbox, and the big bully from down the street just trampled on his sandcastle. He just sits there on the turf like he's had enough of this stupid game.

The Bears' offense is on the field before he can even gather his legs. He walks limply to the sidelines without any expression. The flood of curse words flow toward him and ricochet off his body as though there's nothing left to absorb them.

"He didn't even try," I say quietly among the boiling sea of fans. "He just sat there and gave up."

Before Gordon even reaches his seat, the ball is snapped to the Bears' quarterback, who tosses it nineteen yards to his receiver for a touchdown.

7

The black sky is like a deep hole sucking the stadium bowl dry. Tyler and I get in line with the people filing out. I look at their faces. Fans who had been dancing and shouting now march in silence. As they pass through the exit tunnel, they turn back into factory workers, clerks, and mechanics.

Tyler and I make our way out to the atrium. I look around and notice all the cool banners that are up, I see the faces of old Packers stars glaring triumphantly across the great hall. My stomach drops about an inch lower.

We meet Hank at a restaurant in the stadium. I keep stirring my fries. When Hank buys us a round of ice cream, I just sit there and let it melt. I'm not really sure what's bothering me. It could be the game, but it feels more unusual than that. There's something tugging at my stomach.

Then Tyler says something that I wish I would have. "When are we going home?"

Hank drops his spoon in his empty ice cream bowl. "Don't you want dessert?" he says.

"But we just had dessert."

Hank gets a huge grin, and I know he's got something more up his sleeve.

Tyler and I follow Hank down a maze of hallways below the main level of the stadium. We turn a corner, and I can see a set of dark green double doors at the end.

Hank pulls a key from his pocket, thrusting it into the slot. Then he pries back the right door and reveals the chamber within. I step over the threshold. In that brief moment—a moment with no one else but me in the room—I truly believe that I'm in Heaven.

The room is a large oval, like the shape of the stadium above it. There are some fifty personal dressing stalls lining the outside wall, and each has its own sparkling yellow helmet and silky forest green game-day jersey hanging from a hook as if it had all been professionally prepared. I look down at my feet and notice I'm standing on the edge of a large carpeted G that winds around the brim of the floor and spirals into the center of the Packers' locker room.

Silence. Hank and Tyler trickle in behind me, careful not to move even a single flake of dust in the air.

I remove my hat and place it over my chest. I walk to the center where the tip of the G weaves gently into the fabric, and I take another look around. My mind flashes to the list back at home, stuffed under my mattress. *Take the Packers to the Super Bowl.* This is exactly where I saw myself when I wrote that.

For a moment, I imagine myself standing here in a uniform and my teammates kneeled by my side with their arms wrapped around each other's shoulders, each waiting to hear my words. With unmatched authority, I yell the game plan and get the army ready for the battle of a lifetime. They listen well, and when I finish, I motion for everyone to rise. Together we turn to the tunnel that goes to the field, and I lead my team down it into glory.

I look down the tunnel for real now. It's quiet and dark, but at the end I can see a speck of light from the field.

Maybe I won't ever be suiting up for the big game, but standing here right now, I feel like I could take them all the way.

"Surprised?"

I flinch, forgetting for a moment that there are people here beside me.

"Uh, yeah."

"This is . . . better than ice cream." Tyler says.

Just then Hank's cell phone starts to ring, and I'm surprised that he can get reception from so high up in the clouds. He yanks his phone from its holster and looks at the screen.

"I've gotta take this," he says. "I'll be just a minute." He motions for the door.

"You're leaving us all alone?"

"Explore!" He says. "Try on a jersey! Have some fun!" The door latches shut behind him with a snap that echoes across the hall.

I take a moment to soak it in. The woodwork, the murals on the wall, the lights in the ceiling that seem to warm the entire room. I finally get out my camera and snap a few pictures. "Check this out," I say, and I urge Tyler over to one end of the oval.

"Whoa. That's Gordon Fisher," he gasps, moving in closer to Gordon's locker. He eyes the fabric on the polyester jersey before taking it in between his fingers and rubbing it side to side.

I place my hat down on a nearby bench and look on from the side, poring over the stitching on the name, and the elastic band that wraps around the collar. It's so authentic I can hear it speaking, "Go ahead. Give it a try." The words sound authentic too, like they were coming . . .

. . . from right behind me. I reach over to tug Tyler on the shoulder, but he's already looking.

"Are you Victor?"

I struggle to find words. "Uh . . . yeah . . . Hey, Mr. Fisher." No, it's not a ghost, but Tyler and I each look like we've just seen one. Before I even question if this is real, I realize that the grey hair and light southern twang don't lie.

"Call me Gordon. And you're Tyler?"

"Tyler. Yeah . . . I'm Tyler."

"Pleasure to meet you guys," Gordon says as he takes a seat on the bench near his own stall. Now he's at eye level with me, and still a good ways above Tyler's head. He puts his elbows down on his legs casually, as though he were a normal person. I can't believe it.

Finally I build up the courage. "Uh, Mr. . . . . Gordon? . . . With respect, what are *you* still doing here?"

"You don't want me here?"

"No, it's just—"

"Oh, I get it. All the publicity. Well, I can stay over in the corner—I'll be real quiet if you want!"

"No, Gordon, you're fine!" I say, and regret saying it so loud once I realize that he's smiling.

"Okay, you caught me," he says and throws out his hands. "When I heard Victor and Tyler were gonna be in the locker room, I couldn't help but sneak my way back in."

I manage to laugh at his and my own stupidity. Growing up, I had always seen on TV some of the goofy pranks Gordon had played on his teammates. I guess it was just a shock seeing him here, realizing it was actually him and taking in that he actually has a real personality. I guess famous athletes are people, too.

"So the Foundation had you come here for me?" I ask him.

"You got it. But that doesn't mean at all that I didn't want to be here anyway. I never say no to hanging out with a fan when I get an opportunity."

"Wow. Awesome," I say. My mind flashes back to the day at training camp, Gordon flying past a huge crowd of fans in his SUV. I get a slight uneasy feeling in my gut, but it passes by quickly. "I'm sorry about the game," I say. "We should've won."

Apparently it was the wrong thing to say. Gordon heaves a great sigh, but tries to cover it as best as he can. "Yeah . . . it happens. You can't win 'em all." He looks down and notices my hat sitting on the bench next to him. He welcomes the distraction. "This your hat?" I nod. He picks it up and throws it over his right fist as if his arm were wearing it. "Looks like Sean got to you first," he says, running his finger over Sean's signature. "He told me he ran into you a few weeks back. Bet that was pretty cool."

I look at the hat, too, not really able to look someone in the eye when I've spent so much of my life looking at them through a facemask. "He's a great guy," I say.

"Yeah. One of the best I know." He studies the hat a little more. "Tell me, what's the deal with the brim here? Why's it all cut up like that?"

Tyler takes a tiny step back behind me. With a little chuckle, I help him out and say, "Yeah, it was an accident . . . when I was little, with scissors."

"Careful next time," he says kind of plainly, "wouldn't want to vandalize your team's logo, now."

I smirk, but kind of feel dumb when he says that.

"You want me to sign it too?"

"Yeah, anywhere you want."

"Alright," he says. He takes a thick Sharpie off his belt, which makes me realize this is probably a routine.

"Thanks," I say.

"Can you sign my hat too?" Tyler takes off his crudely constructed paper-mache Cheesehead and offers it to Gordon, who looks a bit hesitant.

"And what happened to yours, then? Chainsaw accident?" Tyler gives a timid grin. Gordon yanks out the Sharpie once more. He finds the flattest part the hat has to offer and gives a jagged sketch of a signature. He tosses it back on Tyler's head, a little bit off kilter, before returning the Sharpie to his belt.

Tyler immediately removes the hat and examines the autograph. He looks like a kid in a candy store, only he wanted chocolate and they gave him butterscotch. "Thanks," he says.

"No problem."

"I just wish it didn't have to come after such a lousy play," he adds.

"What do you mean?" Gordon asks.

"I mean that interception."

"Oh . . . yeah. Well, no big deal. Like I said, it happens."

I can tell that Gordon got a little annoyed by that. I can also tell that Tyler doesn't realize it.

"It's just that it set the record," Tyler adds. "Did you know that?"

"Yeah, I heard."

Tyler goes on. "It must stink having the most in history. But that's okay. You still rock."

My knee starts to rattle from side to side a little bit. I want Tyler to see how irritating he's looking right now. I want him to stop for Gordon's sake, too, but I can't go and say that out loud.

"Yeah, well, we lost the game," Gordon says calmly. "That's my number one concern."

Tyler only continues. "And we probably would have won if that didn't happen—I mean, they scored on the next play."

"Take it easy there, buddy." Gordon's still trying to keep a level voice, but this time it slips a little bit. I get the feeling that he wouldn't mind throwing Tyler into a one-on-one with the Bear's linebacker right about now.

"Sorry," Tyler says.

"I already got enough of a hollering from the press. Don't really need it from you."

"Sorry. I didn't mean to make you angry."

"It's okay, just—"

"I only meant, you know, you could've done better."

Gordon flips his eyes from a blank stare over to the feeble, guiltless pair in Tyler's head. A switch in him flips. "I could've done *better*? How?"

Tyler pivots his ankle awkwardly and looks down at the floor. "Well, I don't know . . . you threw it right to him."

"You don't know what you're talking about. It wasn't my fault." By then I know where this is headed, and I don't think Tyler is ready for it. But I don't know if I'm ready for it either.

I turn to Gordon and say the exact same thing he just said to Tyler, and I'm a little surprised that I did. "Hey, take it easy. He's just a kid."

"Yeah, but he needs to learn a thing or two about manners."

"*What?*"

"You just gotta understand, there's more to a play than just me. My linemen—"

"Your linemen didn't do their job," I say. "So what?"

"Kid, you don't know what you're talking about. I played my a—I played my butt off the whole game. Not one second did I quit."

"Yes, you did."

"What?"

"You did quit for one second. When you threw that pick, you just sat down. But you might've made the tackle if you had kept going."

"What do you mean?"

"I saw the game! You sat down and quit."

"For one second? You're mad at me for supposedly quitting for *one second*, when I could've saved—what, two or three yards? Or maybe *none?*"

"But you don't kn—"

"It wouldn't have been worth it! Anything could have happened—I could've gotten hurt. Any coach would praise me for staying down like I did."

Without realizing it, I've clenched my fists white. I've never heard something so uninspiring. Tyler is now tucked behind me, probably hoping Gordon forgot he was ever there. Between my teeth I say, "You should've tried."

"And killed myself in the act?"

"Yes!" I shout, and the echo bounds off the walls of the oval room. "You don't have many more shots at the Super Bowl. This could be your last year, even. So you've gotta put everything on the line, risk every ounce of your life to make it happen. You've got nothing else to lose."

Gordon hesitates. It looks like he's thinking about the words. Really thinking. But when he speaks, I know he doesn't care. "I think we're about done here," he says. He gets to his feet, but I can't help interrupting.

"I'm not trying to be mean, Gordon. I'm trying to help!" I say this so loud I come to the verge of tears in my eyes.

"Yeah, thanks kid. But I think I can deal with it myself." Gordon makes for one of the exits, clearly agitated. But then again, so am I, and I say something I immediately wish I didn't.

"Obviously not."

He stops. He turns. He looks at me and says, "I don't need this." Then he points a finger lazily at my head. "Now take your stupid hat and get out of here."

Those words break open a dam in my heart. I try to look at him sternly, but the tears in my eyes make it nearly impossible.

I pull the stupid hat from my head by the brim, and I throw it on the floor in front of his feet. I turn, grab Tyler by the shoulder, and head out the door.

My last glance of the locker room is a tiny light in the distance. It's the tunnel that leads to the field. I'll never get the chance to run through it.

TIMEOUT

Eleven Years Earlier

There was a faint glow from the end of the tunnel.

"We ain't in Kansas anymore, Toto," Gordon Fisher said to Elijah White. Gordon had a playful smirk on his face. For Elijah, it was a completely different story. For the last thirteen years of his life, he had fallen short of the big game. Now, he was preparing to run onto the field to face the Patriots in the Super Bowl. Elijah took a moment to reflect. There were so many trials. Working every day of his life to get here today. He knew that the quick, simple run down the tunnel would do no justice to the long journey he had taken to get there.

"Just promise me something," Elijah said, and now he had Gordon's full, sincere attention. He took a deep breath, and said, "Cherish every moment. Take advantage of every opportunity. Win or lose, you'll be a better man in the end."

His name was announced over the loud speaker. It was his time. He strapped on his helmet. He took the first step, then he went to a trot, and finally to a full sprint. As he reached the field, the stadium lights encased his body in a gentle warmth, and Elijah realized that he was one step closer to true glory.

Immediately, he gathered several of his teammates, along with a group of Patriot players, and huddled them in the center of the field, each man leaning on his brother in a painted mix of black and white faces, green and blue jerseys. Elijah took a knee and began to lead them in prayer.

A short while later, Elijah was in his own team's end zone running a light drill for warm-ups. He took a three-point stance across from his own offensive tackle. The coach's whistle blew, and Elijah whipped his left arm over the tackle's helmet and swam right past him. The whistle blew again, and Elijah slowed to a halt. He turned to walk to the back of the line when he was interrupted by a large fan in the end zone's front row.

"Hey Elijah!" the man heckled. "Hey 'Minister,' I got a question. You think you're all holy doin' that prayer before every game? I seen you every time I go to Lambeau, huddled in that circle of yours, and it makes me sick!"

Elijah turned to the man, perturbed. "You got a problem with the way I live?" he hollered.

The fan just scoffed. "We come here to see football! They pay you to sack the quarterback, not to shove that religious crap down our throats!"

"You don't want to see me pray?" Elijah bellowed.

The fan responded, "Hell no!"

Elijah suddenly had the urge to run his next drill with a new target. But he held himself back. Now was not the time to get angry. He just stared the man down and said, "Then I suggest you don't come to the games anymore."

He kept eye contact with the man all the way to the back of the line, and he turned away and continued his warm-ups, taking his mind off the fan immediately.

No one knows what became of that lone obnoxious fan. But that night, Elijah made sure that his own name was never forgotten. During the game, he recorded three quarterback sacks—the most in Super Bowl history.

To end the night, he took the beautiful sterling silver trophy in his hand and hoisted it high above his head. His bright smile reflected brightly off the lights, and warmed the stadium.

This is it. I've finally arrived.

He turned to Gordon and put the trophy in his friend's hands. As he let go, he told Gordon one last time, "Cherish every moment."

MATTHEW NEBEL

3RD QUARTER: LOOKING FOR A STRONG FOUNDATION

MATTHEW NEBEL

8

"Are you sad?"

I shake my head.

Dad and Mom are sitting by my bedside in two wooden chairs from the kitchen. It's way past midnight, and my puffy red past-midnight eyes show it. Curled with my knees to my chin, I rub my hands across my cheeks and feel the crusty residue of a night's worth of tears. No, I'm not crying anymore. Once in a while I quiver uncontrollably or suck in a funnel of air, and it all makes me look like I'm crying. It's been over an hour since I looked into their eyes. I just look at the wall.

"Are you still upset over what happened?"

I shake my head.

"It's okay if you're upset."

"It's not what happened at the game," I say. My throat feels like a cold, dry mine shaft. I quiver and suck in three more funnels of air before continuing.

"There's something I've been thinking about for a long time."

I think about the silent ride back from the game. We were *silent* in a *limousine* after a free ticket to *Lambeau Field*. If those things couldn't make me happy, what could?

My parents are silent—just what I was afraid of.

Finally, I admit it to them. "I feel like none of it matters."

They're still silent. I don't know for sure, but it feels like they're looking at each other.

"What do you mean when you say that?" Dad says.

"I . . . I just don't see the point of it all. Anything. School, work, friends, fun . . . it just seems like none of it really matters."

Dad wipes his face. "Now, why would you say something like that?"

"Because it's the way I feel. I feel like none of this really matters. I mean, if we're all gonna die anyway, then it doesn't make any difference how your life goes, or what you do, or how many friends you have or how much money you make, or how happy you are. It all just becomes . . . a waste.

"I mean, even if you go to Heaven or something afterward, doesn't that make life on Earth just a big waiting room? I . . . I just feel scared that I can go through life without even knowing what the point is, and then in the end, realize that it didn't matter anyway."

I finally look their way, and I shuffle my feet. Mom has barely said anything all night. Dad looks like he's thinking hard about what to say.

He takes a breath. "You want to know something, Victor?" he says. "We're scared too."

I never thought that was possible until now.

"So . . . we're all scared, then?" I ask. I look around the room, and for the first time, I feel like I'm just as old as them. Dad nods his head. I turn to Mom, but she's looking away. The sleeve of her sweater is splotchy with tears.

I think back. What was it she told me again? Live like I know I need to? Maybe she's telling herself the same thing right now. She's thinking through her words, and trying to find the best thing to say, just like Dad.

But then she doesn't speak. And more time goes by. And she still doesn't speak.

"Mom?" I ask.

And again she says nothing. Slowly, she gets up and walks out of the room, leaving me and Dad stranded. A few seconds later, I hear a door close shut in the hallway.

I don't open my eyes right away when I wake up. The air is even colder than the day before. I'm not going to school today. I tell Dad I don't feel good, and he doesn't ask any questions.

By seven thirty, the apartment is clear of all grown-ups. Dad's at work and Mom's out of town visiting a friend, which means I've got the place to myself.

For a while I just lie in bed, wasting more time—only this time I'm aware of it. Then I get up and leave my room, skipping over the bathroom, the toothbrush, and the shower to head straight for the kitchen.

Halfway down the hall I notice I'm still wearing my clothes from last night. I must not have bothered to take them off. Once in the kitchen, I yank a few drawers open to make a little staircase up to the counter so I can open the cupboard. Inside there is a sea of depressed food; half-eaten boxes of cereal, expired cans of soup, and a few random jars of artichoke something-or-other.

I reach for a box of Pop Tarts, but there's only one package left inside. I hop down from the counter, head over to the toaster, and peel back the foil to look at my breakfast—two stale squares of sugar. I look over to the kitchen table to think about the breakfast buffet I had yesterday. I decide that happiness doesn't matter if you can feel so happy one day and so unhappy the next. I think about how great it would be if people could store their happiness in little tokens, so if one day they got so happy that they didn't need it all, they could save the leftovers and spend them later.

The long morning rolls into the afternoon. I head to the front closet and throw on my shoes and a light jacket. I think a short walk might be what I need to clear my head.

The air outside feels crisp. The park is just a few blocks away, so I should get back before either of my parents get home from work. The frost is mostly gone now, but my shoes still get stained with water as I start out across the lawn. As I walk, I notice how withered the grass looks. Even on other people's lawns, the grass is growing the color of moldy bread.

It's sad. It's like the winter isn't quite yet here, but it has sent some of its soldiers ahead to make sure we know that it's coming. And everything—the grass, the trees, the dirty streets and cars—just sort of lay down their weapons and give in. It's sad, but what's even worse is knowing that all *those* things will come back to life next spring.

Two older ladies are out for a walk. I keep my head tilted low with my hands in my coat pockets as we cross paths, but they still say hi with big smiles on their faces, so I say hi back.

A string of cars lines the curbside leading up to the park. I turn onto the walkway next to the forest line and keep on thinking. I think more about winter, how it keeps everyone inside. It keeps people together. But somehow we still manage to keep out of each other's way. I think about how Christmas brings us together and Christmas is in the winter.

But Christmas doesn't really bring us together.

I imagine me and my family sitting in the living room while we all exchange gifts. My parents are laughing because I've flung wrapping paper high in the air and scattered it everywhere. It all falls to the floor and creates a maze in the room, blocking us from ever finding each other. I imagine smashing all of the presents in the world, so people would have nothing left to look at but each other, and they would have to give each other answers.

I hear a game whistle blow in the distance, and I turn my head right. There's a peewee football game on the other side of the park. I step off the path and walk a little closer, until I get to a tall chain link fence. I take my hands out of my pockets and put them on the fence, and just watch for a little while.

I picture myself back in fourth grade. I'm in the uniform, strapped into my helmet and I can hear each heartbeat in my head. I'm at linebacker. The opposing running back is scrawny, and his legs begin to shake as he anticipates the coming snap. He receives the ball. I see an open lane off the right guard, and I take full charge. Before he can see me, I strike like lightning and he is tossed horizontal in the air. The ball carelessly falls to the ground, and I jump on top of it.

Now I'm in fifth grade. I'm in the uniform, strapped into my helmet, and I can hear each heartbeat my head. I'm at linebacker. Across the way is my enemy. I try to muster up a grimace that might scare him off, but all I see looking back at me under the helmet are two dark phantom-like eyes. He's waiting for me. He can smell me. He knows something that I don't know. The ball is snapped and handed off to the phantom. Suddenly my legs become very heavy, like they're stuck in the ground. I squirm and squirm with all my might, but I can't break free. I see a lane open up off the right guard, and he takes full charge. He's coming straight at me. He tucks his shoulder low and plunges headfirst into my chest, and shatters my heart.

The whistle blows again. The field, I notice, is even more torn up than the grass around it. Huge metal light posts surround the field, and it takes me back to a forgettable memory. The whistle blows, and there's Tyler and me in the crowd at Lambeau Field. Gordon lines up under center, and he turns to look at us. He tells me this next play is dedicated in my honor. He takes the snap and tells the linemen to stand down. He keeps a firm smirk on his face, looking straight at me as thousands of defenders plunge at him and bury him alive.

I look at the light posts again and think about the lights at Lambeau Field, about how they're all frauds because they don't light up anything important. Maybe Mom knows that, and that's why she's so sad. That's gotta be it. She's realized what I just recently realized, that all the work she put into bringing the lights to the field doesn't actually matter.

I think about the soapbox racer, about how that stupid hunk of junk is trying to make me feel like a bad person all because I won't spend time with it. Then I think about Tyler and how his stupid dad and uncles mistreat him. I think about how he won't ever tell anyone because he doesn't have any confidence in himself. A lot of people would say he's brave because he's gone through so much crap in his life being small and weak and picked on and stuff. But he's not brave, and neither am I. Just going through crap in life doesn't make you brave. And if you ever get sick, and you can't get a transplant, and your heart stops working, and you die, that doesn't mean you were brave either. It just means that something lousy happened to you, and you couldn't do anything about it.

The whistle blows again. I hear the faint cheer of a small crowd of moms. I move my head in closer to the fence, and see that one of the teams on the field is mine. Well not mine, but my friends' team. I see everyone's parents and our coach. I dip down a little lower so I won't get spotted. I look at the jerseys and single out Randy. Another memory races back to me.

Randy and I were out in his backyard last summer. He had just gotten a new dog—a chocolate lab—and we had this tennis ball that was all mangled up and deflated. So we decided to play monkey in the middle with this ball and his dog. Two hours. That's how long we played, and we only stopped because it got dark before we were done. I can't remember why I thought it was so much fun, but it was. Maybe that's the whole point of life: trying to be satisfied. But maybe that's just a way to cover up the fact that there isn't any point.

I let go of the fence and tuck my hands back into my coat and turn back. I think about how happy they all must be if they win, how sad they must be if they lose. I think about how they're probably going out for pizza afterward and they're all going to have a great time, but tomorrow they'll be no better off than they were today. I think about how they don't even realize that their lives are ticking clocks.

The sun is burning orange and blue. The shadow it casts behind me is five times my height, and for a second I think it's the phantom chasing after me. A cold nip at my face makes me hunch down into the collar of my jacket, and the wind on my eyes helps me hold back a few tears.

I walk into the front door just after sunset. Dad's in the kitchen and Mom's on the couch reading. I brush off my face with the inside collar of my jacket, and I hang it up in the closet. Immediately, I notice something's different with the attitude around home. No one seems to care that I'm home, or that I've been gone. Mom just keeps her nose tightly in her book. I peek into the kitchen as I'm passing by into the hallway. Dad's putting dishes away. He and I make eye contact, and he nods to me.

I turn the corner and head into my room, closing the door and deciding to leave the light off. The deep blue of the sky is enough for me to find my bed. I lie down and begin to think about how weird it is, that so much has happened to me in the past few months—I've done so much, too—but still I'm right back in this bed where I started. I remember my teacher last year talked about displacement, the distance that you move over a certain amount of time. I guess my displacement over the past few months is zero.

9

I wake up the following morning, Tuesday, and it seems like nothing has changed. All I can look forward to is an echo of yesterday. I hear the doorknob turn, and I quickly turn over on my side to make it look like I was sleeping. I knew it was Dad coming in, cause he's the only one who's even noticed me the past few days. But even he has only just noticed me.

He walks over and takes a seat on the end of my bed. I hear my "Before I Die" list crinkle beneath him. He wipes his five o'clock shadow, takes a sip of his coffee, and says, "How we doing today, champ?"

"Not so well," I say and curl into the fetal position like a helpless little critter.

"Not so well, huh?" He sighs. "You know, Vic, you can't go on like this forever. I know we kind of had a freebie day yesterday, but today you've gotta go to school."

"No, I really don't feel so well." I pull the pillow around the back of my head, as if it will make a blockade from Dad.

"Victor. I'm not going to listen to any of it. Come on, get out of bed, jump in the shower and get some clean clothes on. I mean it."

"What's the point? We don't even do anything in class. I'll go tomorrow."

Dad rubs his face again. I feel like I've made a valid statement. What is the point? It's not like I'm going to use anything I learn in math later in life.

"Victor," he says, "I understand you're not happy right now, but that doesn't mean you can just give up." He takes a kinder tone. "You're going to have to tough this one out, even though it's hard." He doesn't say anything more than that. He just looks me in the eye then pats my knee through the blanket and walks out of the room.

The shower feels better than I had expected. And the warm toast and honey is better than the Pop Tarts I had yesterday. I feel like it might be an okay day after all, but I don't want to admit it out loud.

I meet up with Tyler in the hallway before school starts. He looks a little flustered.

"How are you feeling?" I say.

"Kind of tired," he says, and he rubs his eyes.

"I meant since the game."

"Oh," he looks off to the side. "I don't know."

"Not so good?"

"No, not really."

"I'm sorry."

"It's okay. It's not your fault, and it's not really that big of a deal."

He shuffles uneasily. I don't think he truly believes that in his heart, but I don't need to push it any further. Plus, I've got something different on my mind.

"What do you say we get back to work on that racer?"

He looks up, and his eyes are wide.

"There's still more than a month left until the race," I say. "We could get started today after school."

"I can't today."

"Why not?"

"I've got piano lessons."

"Oh, right. Tuesday."

The bell rings, and people start shuffling around us.

"But Victor," he says.

"Yeah?"

"We could do it tomorrow, if you want?"

"Tomorrow? I don't know . . ." I pretend to check an imaginary planner. "I only have openings for the rest of forever." I flip the imaginary book closed. Tyler smiles, and I give him a pat on the back, then he turns and heads down the third grade hall.

"We'll talk tomorrow," I say.

Back in my own class, Jared and Randy bludgeon me with questions that I don't want to answer. Thankfully, I'm saved by the bell. Ms. Sherman enters the room, and the class quiets down. As she begins the lesson I glance over at Randy, but quickly turn back. I feel like asking him if he remembers the time we played fetch with his dog. Maybe I'll bring it up later. Maybe I won't. It's not that big of a deal.

When I pull up to the apartment, there's a dark sports car I've never seen before parked outside. Either Mom and Dad won the lottery, or we've got company over.

I jump off my bike still in motion, and I let it coast its way toward the yard until it crashes on a clump of dirt, and I head inside.

I turn to meet Mom, Dad and—I wasn't expecting him. It's Sean Driver. He's in my living room eating snacks and chatting with my parents like they've been friends all their lives.

"How's it going, big guy?" Sean asks, shining a smile that could warm the world.

"Good," I answer, cause that's all I can muster up to say. Give me a few seconds more, though, and I brilliantly ask, "How are you?"

"I'm doing just fine. Just stopped by after practice, hoping to find you."

"But how come?"

He motions to the coffee table and nudges the jagged-brimmed autographed Packer hat that I had left on the floor of the locker room. I hadn't even thought about it since then.

I feel my face flush red.

"Sean said he was very angry when he found out you didn't want his autograph after all," Mom jokes.

I manage a half-hearted laugh. It's the first time Mom has talked to me in two days, and I'm a little surprised that she decided to snap the record-breaking streak by telling a joke.

Maybe it's the occasion that's got her all playful. Maybe she actually wanted to talk all along, and that was the easiest way to start.

Sean stays well into the night, with Dad asking him questions about the team, and Mom chiming in to ask about her favorite players. Later in the evening, though, Sean and I head outside to walk around the block. We hunch over with our hands in our coat pockets.

"Okay," I say, "so what's the real reason you came over? It doesn't take that long to return a hat."

"I just wanted to see how you were doing," he says.

"Well, there's still no donor for a heart transplant."

"That's not what I meant." He looks at me, and I can see the glint of the glowing orange streetlamps in his eyes. "I wanted to see if you were doing okay after the game. I got there just after you left, and that disappointed me a little bit. I was talking to Gordon, and he told me what happened."

"Oh. Yeah, I'm doing okay. I guess."

"You were angry though, when it happened."

"Yeah, I guess I was angry. I mean, I threw my hat down, but that was just kind of a heat-of-the-moment thing."

"In the heat of the moment, we can be our most honest."

We turn the corner and the wind starts to whip lightly in our faces. I breathe onto my hands and rub some warmth back into my ears.

He continues, "I just wanted to apologize for what happened. Gordon doesn't act like that ever. If you knew him, you'd know I was telling the truth. He just . . . The thing you have to understand about him is that he's super competitive. In everything. He has to win. So after we lost that game, I think he just got a little wound up. Especially in a game like that where we should've won . . . that's no excuse though. The way he acted was out of line. So I'm sorry that that happened."

"Thanks, I appreciate that," I say. "But if you talked to him, and he says he feels bad, then why didn't he come to apologize?"

Sean shuffles in his coat. "I . . . I can't tell you that. Again, he's competitive. I think he just has a little too much pride right now."

"Oh, great. That makes me feel better."

"Well, we *all* have issues with pride. Would you agree with that?"

But then I think back to the start of the school year. I didn't stick up for Tyler. I even ditched him for my other friends once.

"Yeah. I guess," I say.

"Now, that doesn't mean he shouldn't apologize. I think he just works differently than most people."

We turn the corner again.

"You remember what I told you the day we first met at training camp?" he asks, "That even the smallest thing you do can make a huge difference?"

"Yeah . . . I remember."

"So, what have you been doing to make a difference?"

I shuffle a little bit.

"I guess I've been a better friend to Tyler lately," I say. "But I don't know. I haven't been doing anything else. I guess it's just . . . hard . . . to believe."

"Believe what?"

"That what I do will actually matter in the end. It's hard when you can't see the result right away."

"I gotcha," he says and pauses for a moment. "So let me ask you this; is it worth doing something good even if you don't get something back in return?"

"Well, I guess it still does good in the world."

"Exactly. There are examples all over the world of exactly what you're talking about, like Martin Luther King Jr."

"I learned about him in school," I say.

"Good, good. So you know how hard he fought to get rights for black people like me, then?"

"Yeah, I mean, like I said, I read about it. I know he took a huge risk in fighting for rights, and that he put himself in danger for it. I don't know everything about him though."

"But you know he was killed."

"Yeah . . ."

"And he was killed *because* of the good things he did."

"Yeah. That made me pretty sad. He never got to see how racism is gone now."

Sean presses a hand to my shoulder. "Careful before you say that, Victor. It's not gone yet. It's far from gone."

"What? No one I know is racist."

He sighs. "Unfortunately, it still happens."

I look down at the tiles of sidewalk as they pass beneath my feet. I feel bad for saying something so stupid. "Sorry I said that. I guess I knew it was still going on."

"It's true," he says, "but there's also some beauty to it when you think about it."

"What?"

"Dr. King gave up his life to fight for equality. And he made such a big impact that the things he did way back then are still changing what goes on today. We're living it right now, and that means we're keeping his dream alive."

"Yeah," I say, "I guess that is pretty cool." I pause, and the only sound comes from our shoes clomping on the sidewalk. Then, it all finally clicks together for me. "So what you're saying is that I should keep trying to make a difference."

"Exactly! Just like I said, even the smallest action can change the world."

For the first time, I consider that every action has a consequence, and we will never know what would have happened if we had done things differently. I think of how I never would have met Sean if he hadn't left his shoe in the locker room, and none of this would have happened, and I'd probably be in bed at home right now, with a displacement of zero. But it didn't happen that way. Sean *did* forget his shoe and I *did* meet him, and he *is* standing here right now making me realize all of this in the first place.

Sean goes on. "So, you said you've been a good friend to Tyler lately, right? I'll bet that's made a big difference in his life."

"I guess," I say.

I think about Tyler and how he doesn't get much attention at school or at home. I think about how I've learned to be a good friend because of my parents. Does that mean in the long run that they've helped make Tyler's life a little better? I guess it does. After all, Martin Luther King Jr. never knew Sean, but he sure made Sean's life better.

"I just realized something," I say. "I haven't been getting along with my parents the best lately. But maybe it's not all their fault."

"Uh huh," he says, listening.

"I probably could be treating them better. I mean, I figure that they're probably going through a hard time right now just like I am. I didn't realize it until just now."

Sean nods his head. "That's good," he says.

"But that's a whole other story, with my parents. I think I can figure that one out on my own."

"I'm sure your parents are proud of you. You might just not realize it yet."

"Proud? I haven't really done anything to deserve that."

"When I was talking with them earlier, they said you had. They said you are always looking to do the right thing." I shuffle in my jacket a little bit. "I think a quality like that is contagious."

"Thanks."

"So now do you believe you can make a difference?"

"Yeah, I do."

"Good, because that's the entire reason I brought all this up. About Gordon."

Gordon. I had completely forgotten that that's where this conversation had begun.

Sean goes on. "I think that night in the locker room really meant something to him."

"Yeah, I'll bet," I scoff.

"No, I'm serious," Sean says. "The fact that he mentioned it means that it's on his mind. That's just one more link in the chain reaction."

"So you think what I said may have actually changed him?"

Sean sighs. "Man, I can't tell you that."

"Oh."

"Hey, don't look so down now," he says lightly. "What did we just learn?"

"That a small thing can make a huge difference."

"Yeah, but it can also take a long time to see the results."

When I lie back in bed that night—in the same spot where I woke up this morning—I realize that even though I have learned so much today, I have still made a displacement of zero. Maybe there can be progress in life, even when it looks like there isn't any.

10

I pick Tyler up with my bike on the way to school the next morning. He rides on the back pegs while gripping my shoulders and huddles behind my head to hide from the wind. Of course he was excited when I told him about Sean coming over to my house, but I had something else on my mind, and I couldn't wait to say it.

"So Tyler," I say. "You remember what the representative guy from the Dream Foundation said?"

"Hank?"

"Yeah. When we met he said it's important to appreciate the short time we have. He was talking about the short ride we had in the limo, but I think he was also talking about the short time we have on Earth."

Tyler doesn't respond.

"Anyway, that stuck with me. It's this whole thing with trying to find meaning in life . . . I know you don't really understand or care—"

"No, I care."

"Really?"

"Yeah."

"Great. It's kind of hard to tell sometimes, if people actually care, you know? Anyway, I've been trying for a while now to find an answer to how I can make my life matter. But after thinking last night and this morning, I think I've got a good plan. I want to start my own charity; one that will help kids really do good in the world."

I wait for a response, but Tyler stays quiet, and that makes me nervous.

"It wouldn't be anything big, or anything," I say, "I just want to help kids achieve their dreams."

"What about the Dream Foundation?" he says.

I hunch my shoulders low. "The Dream Foundation is great," I say, "But they're all about having something happen *to* you. When I think of following my dreams, I think of *doing* something and *achieving* something. I think people really want to make the world better."

Tyler takes a moment, then a moment longer. Then he says, "I think it's a perfect idea."

I'm relieved. My biggest goal right off the bat was to find someone who didn't think it was completely stupid. I considered asking my parents for help first, but—

"What do your parents think about it?"

"Well . . . I still have a few wrinkles to iron out with my parents. They'll find out on their own time, don't worry."

"Are you sure *that's* a perfect idea?"

"No."

"Okay then."

"We'll do fine on our own," I say. "I'll be president. You can be vice-president or something." Tyler shivers a little bit, which I can feel since his hands are gripping my shoulders.

We come up to the school, and I bike around to the bike racks in the back. I lock up my bike, and we head for the door.

"So when are we going to get started?" Tyler asks.

"We could start today after school. The first thing we need to do is go to the bank to open an account."

"That won't work, though."

"Why?"

"We wouldn't have enough time. Banks close earlier than other stores."

"Are, are you sure?"

"Yeah, pretty sure."

I hold the back door open and let a few second-graders in, then Tyler and I follow. We walk by the main office, the principal's office, and the nurse's room. Tyler glances at each one. "But maybe we could go before they close, anyway," he says.

"What do you mean?"

"I've got an idea, too."

The note clenched in my hand has a sketchy forged signature on it, but my bigger fear is that it will become even more smudged from the sweat in my hand.

Dear Ms. Sherman, Victor needs to be taken out of class today at lunchtime for a doctor's appointment. Smooth, and so original, too.

The more I think about it, the more I'm surprised that Tyler was able to easily convince me to do this. Maybe he's become a little more daring than I give him credit for. A thought passes through my mind of him in the third-grade wing right now, just casually handing his slip to the teacher with a smile, and then moonwalking his way out of the classroom. I catch myself feeling jealous, even though it's not even real.

I walk up to Ms. Sherman, who's sitting politely at her desk reading a local section of the *Press-Gazette*.

"Hello, Victor," she says, "How's your morning going?"

My legs start shaking. For a split second, I consider turning around and scrubbing the whole operation. Then I think of Tyler and how he's no longer moonwalking but shivering alone outside by the bike racks, and he's cursing my name.

"I . . . er, here's this," I say. I stupidly hold out the dampened paper. She looks at me curiously, then takes the paper and opens up the crease. It briefly reminds me of the list at home.

Live like I know I need to.

Given the situation, I wonder if I'm following that, or going against it.

I watch Ms. Sherman's eyes inspect the slip, and she gets a weird dimple in her cheek where you can't tell if it's suspicion, interest, or just nothing. It's that split second when your heart decides to take a vacation in your throat. All is still, and my mind is blank, but it finally passes.

"Well, I guess we'll see you tomorrow, then." Holding out the slip, she leans forward and whispers, "Don't worry about the homework, if that helps. We'll find a way around it."

Her words are kind, but they feel like ice. "Thanks," I say. I take the slip and turn to my desk in the back. I think Randy and Jared are next to me when I sit down, but I really don't take the time to notice. I feel awful, and there's a pit in my stomach that's sinking my entire body. She was nice. Maybe I could have told the truth, and she would have understood.

At 11:30, our class is released.

"C'mon, Vic." Randy calls after me. "Pizza day, dude."

I don't really feel like talking right now. I get up and walk toward the door. "Uh, you go ahead. Save me a seat with Jared . . . gotta take a whiz." Randy shrugs and turns left into the hall. I turn right.

The next thing I know, the back door is closed behind me, and I'm outside. It's so quiet. I don't think I've ever been out here with nobody else around. Tyler isn't even here.

Then I feel cold, but not from the air. Moments go by— precious moments that each matter because each moment is one in which I could be seen—and I want to get out of here.

C'mon Tyler.

I hear a rustle in the hedges near the sidewalk. I turn my head, and see a small hand beckoning me over.

I crouch over. "Tyler? Let's get going."

Quietly, he pops out of the hedges and jumps onto my back pegs. I kick off my feet, and ride away, tempted to look back. It all felt too easy.

Taking only back roads, we get to the bank in about five minutes. It's the one near my apartment.

We walk inside and find a line of people weaving between the tables. The end of the line is right at the door where we stand.

"At least we got a good view of the outdoors." Tyler waves his hand toward the glass door behind us, out into the busy streets. It's then that I notice the sign on the door. It states the bank's hours in plain white letters.

"Oh," Tyler says. Apparently he sees it too. "Six o'clock." He turns to me with a guilty face, but I shrug it off. I'm more concerned that any one of these adults could know who we are.

"This is gonna take an hour," I whisper. "We're gonna get seen by someone by then."

"It won't take that long. Look, the line is already moving." I turn and see that he's right. The line is moving: very, very slowly.

We stir and slouch and mosey our way toward the front of the line for a half hour. When there's one person ahead of us, I start to get really hot under my shirt—the same way I did when I handed the note to Ms. Sherman. I yank on the collar a few times to let some air in.

"What's wrong?" Tyler asks.

"I just don't know what I'm gonna say."

"Just be honest."

"What do you mean?"

"Just say you wanna start a charity."

"Next!" The young lady calls us up to the counter. She looks nice, like her long dark hair was woven just to fit with her black suit. The heat starts to leave my body, but when she smiles and says her first words, my heart stops beating.

"And what can I do for you little youngsters today?"

But she says it a little too sweetly, and I feel like a puppy. I say nothing, and she looks to the crowd of others behind us waiting in line. She smiles to them, like she's saying "I'll be with you real people in a moment."

"Can I help you with anything?" She says.

I step forward. I'm in the spotlight of the bank, now, so I've got to make a move. I squeak, "We'd like to open an account."

"An account," she says in a half question, half statement.

I clear my throat. "Yes."

She keeps smiling, and leans over the counter so she's closer to our height. "Okay, well, then all we need is for you to come back with your parents and have them fill out a few forms for us." The words hook me by the stomach and swirl my insides around. I look at Tyler, but he doesn't look back. He just stares at the floor and swivels his foot back and forth.

I look back at the bank teller. "Really?"

"That's all we need," she says.

I look down to the floor, and I only speak a few more words. "Thank you for your time." My chin is starting to shake. I need to get out of there before I make myself look stupid. I take Tyler by the shoulder, leading him along because he won't look up to see where he's going. We leave the comfort of the building and burst into the bright, hot sunlight.

Later we're sitting on a curb outside a gas station, eating some hot dogs with two cans of Coke. With each bite and swallow, I wonder where the food is actually going, because I can't feel anything in my stomach.

Lambeau Field is across the street, and the parking lot is empty. Again it reminds me of a castle, a fortress that only lets a select few enter. Then Tyler asks me a question.

"Hey Vic."

"Yeah?"

He takes a giant bite out of his hot dog and says with his mouth full, "Do you think there's football in Heaven?"

I only keep looking across the street, not at the stadium anymore—just at nothing. I'm finished eating, and my cardboard tray is sitting empty beside me. I hold it down so it doesn't blow away in the wind. He turns to look at me and swallows his last bite.

"I've been thinking," he says. "If Heaven has all the stuff you could ever want, there's gotta be sports, right?" I give a slight nod but don't really want to. "So there's gotta be football. I mean, maybe everybody wins every game when you're up there."

"That's stupid," I say.

"Why's it stupid?"

I sigh. "It takes all the fun out of it. There can't be sports if everybody *wins*—it would just be boring. That means everybody loses, too."

"But nobody loses."

"Never mind. Yeah, I guess it's possible."

We sit there a little while longer before getting up to toss out our garbage. I get on my bike and he climbs on the back pegs, holding onto my shoulders as I start toward his house.

"How do you think it happens when you die?" he asks. There's a slight breeze waving our hair around, but I can still hear him fine.

"I don't know. I don't know if I wanna talk about it," I say.

"Oh," he says back, "cause I've kind of got this idea. It's kind of dumb, but I was thinking about what's gonna happen to you . . . and if it's, like, gonna hurt or anything." I'm getting irritated, but I don't tell him. He needs me to listen, and I need him to talk. "And I thought something up last night when I was lying in bed. Something I think you'll like."

"Yeah? Let's hear it."

"Okay." I can feel him take a gulp and begin. "So here's how I see it happening. You're lying there on your bed, and all your family's around you. They're saying goodbye, but they're not sad, they're happy. They're happy cause they know where you're headed."

I know when he says "you," he's not referring to me specifically. He means people in general. But it's still kind of weird to hear him talking like that.

He keeps on going as we round a corner, and his hands clench my shoulders a little tighter. "Everything starts to go white," he says, "and you're fading away from the world, but you're not afraid. You wake up surrounded by a weird white mist. But as things become clearer, you notice where you actually are."

"Where are you?" I ask.

"Promise you won't laugh?"

"No."

"Shut up!"

"Okay, I won't laugh."

He leans in closer to my ear and says, "You're at Lambeau Field."

I don't know what to think, so I say nothing and let him go on. "You're in the team's locker room. The clouds go away but everything's still white, and you feel . . . what's the word . . . weird."

"Surreal?" I ask.

"Yeah, surreal. You feel all surreal, and kind of like you're in a dream, only it's all happening. You turn your head and see that the closest stall has your name on it. There's a jersey in there, and they want you to put it on."

"Who does?"

"The players. They're all there to send you off."

"That's kind of weird." I tell him. We're at his house now, and he jumps off my back. I throw my bike down on the front lawn. We both take a seat on the front steps.

"Yeah, I know it's weird," he says, "but there's more to it than that." By this time, I'm actually interested in what he has to say. He goes on. "You see, you throw on the jersey and get suited up for the game. Your eyes come to the entrance to the tunnel, and you meet an angel there."

"An angel? Angels are Packer fans?"

"Oh yeah, the greatest!" he shouts. Even he gets a sarcastic kick out of it. "He's wearing a Packer jersey too—a beautiful white Packer jersey."

"White's not one of our home jersey colors," I say. "White's not even a color."

"This is *my* imagination, remember?" he scowls. "That's just how the jerseys are in Heaven." I give in and let him finish telling his story. I actually like what he has to say by this point. It's weird, but it's comfortable.

He's on his feet now, facing me still sitting there on the porch.

"So the angel is there. And he reaches out and offers you a hand." Tyler raises his own hand to an imaginary person beside him to demonstrate. "He tells you everything's going to be okay, so you take his hand, and he turns you so you face the tunnel. You can hear the fans now—millions of them—but you can't see them yet, cause the white clouds are blocking your view. The fans keep screaming. They're ready for you. In fact, they've been waiting their whole lives. As you run down the tunnel, hand-in-hand with the angel, the sound of the cheers starts to take over all of your senses, and you disappear into the white light."

He stops. I can tell that he's done because he looks at me expectantly.

"That's good," I say. I really do mean it this time. "You think that's what's going to happen?" I ask.

Tyler thinks for a minute and says, "I don't really know. It was just something I made up."

"Yeah," I say. I look up into the sky and see that clouds are starting to form.

11

Tyler takes out his key and opens the side entry door to the garage. I follow him in with my bike and pop it over the threshold.

"Can't we open up the garage door?" I say.

"Nope, can't risk it. You know how neighbors are. Old Hendrickson across the street's got my dad on speed dial." The Hendricksons live in my former house. I guess everything would be easier if I had never moved.

Tyler goes over to the opposite wall and flips on the single orange light that hangs alone in the center of the room. It's dim and it's dusty, but it'll get the job done. I help Tyler dig the racer skeleton from the corner, and we plop it down in the center of the garage.

"Okay," he says, "There are still several weeks until the race. We're still in pretty good shape, actually, if we can finish the frame by today. You got the plans?"

I dig into the front pocket on my backpack and try to yank out the paper. One of the folded corners tears at the crease after getting caught on the zipper, nearly ripping off completely. I shrug my left shoulder and offer out the serrated paper. Tyler takes it carefully and rubs it flat on his knee.

"We won't need that part," I say.

Tyler squints his eyes and holds the paper up to the orange light. "Yeah, who needs wheels?"

I laugh a little as I turn to go find the drill.

Just after 3:30 p.m., a *chunk* sound comes from the ceiling and the garage door starts to roll up, revealing the front of the sporty BMW. Mike hops out of the car.

"Oh, hey there fellas!" he says. Tyler keeps his eyes buried in the lumber that's sprawled across the floor in front of him. Then Mike turns to me. "Victor, you've become a stranger to us! What's up, buddy?"

I give a smile. "It's all good," I say.

"Well, let's keep it that way. Don't want those so-called teachers knocking you around, telling you what to do." I give half a laugh, but keep my focus on the wooden beam in my hand.

Then he's cut off by another call on his phone. He reaches for his belt and flips it open to look at the caller ID. "Bah, I can take this later." He flips it shut and throws it back in its holster. For the first time, Tyler looks up. "Looks like your car's coming along pretty well. If you guys need any help, you know where to find me."

"Well, actually we do need some plywood cut," Tyler says.

"Perfect," he says, "Let me just go inside for a few minutes, and I'll be right back out." He smiles, but by that time Tyler has already slumped his head back downward. The smile withers from his face, and Mike heads through the door into the kitchen.

When the door closes I stop working and look over at Tyler. It's a few seconds before he realizes that his hammer is the only thing that's making any noise. He nervously raises his head and meets my eyes.

"What?" he says.

"Nothing," I say. I lower my head and he does the same, then, slowly, both hammers join together in harmony.

Thirty minutes later, with the table saw still waiting in the corner, a second car pulls slowly into the driveway. I don't pay it any mind because I figure it's Sarah, but the footsteps I hear are heavy. I turn my head, and so does Tyler.

It's Dad. And that can only mean one thing: school's back in session.

I struggle to find my first words. "Uh, hey—hey Dad." His face is like stone, but it's so warm that you can see it becoming molten; you can feel the heat on your body. I'm suddenly reminded of the last time he wore that same face. I was dragged out of my sleeping bag and into the car.

"Get in the car," he says, as if on cue, and spares me no second glance as he walks past me and up to the door. He knocks.

I quickly tell Tyler goodbye and good luck with nothing more than a raise of the eyebrows, and I flee into the car.

From inches above the dashboard, I peek my head out to see if there's any commotion. So far Tyler is sitting right where he has been all afternoon. He's not working or doing anything, he just looks completely spaced out, and I can't tell if he's thinking really deeply or not at all.

Then Dad returns. He marches through the garage and back to the car. In the doorway behind him stands Mike, looking a little more cool-headed, though still very serious. Tyler gets called inside, and we lock eyes. He looks like he'd rather be me right now, but I can hardly even stand the anticipation of the verbal whomping I'm about to get.

As Dad and I peel out of the driveway, I get one last glance at the racer. Still bare, frail and unstable, for a moment I imagine it calling my name, begging me not to leave it behind.

And then there's silence. Long and painful. Stupidly, I decide to talk first.

"How was school today?" I say, then I instantly regret it.

"I could ask you the same thing," he says.

Before he finishes, I roll my eyes and make a mocking *I could ask you the same thing* in my head. I guess I deserve to be talked to like that, but I can't let myself know that I know that. Pushing my already-empty tank of luck even further down Disaster Road, I say, "Wh—what do you mean?"

I watch his face, trying to keep mine straight and innocent. Then a piston blows under the hood of the car. That must be it, because that's the only thing that could make the world shake and scream so strongly.

"I can't believe you thought you could get away with it! But that isn't even what ticks me off the most, Victor. It's not even that you decided it would be *better* for your life if you skipped school. What really ticks me off is that you did three selfish things."

I can only think of one, and I doubt he knows what it is unless he can read the thoughts in my head—and maybe he can.

"First," he says "you took advantage of your friend. You're ten, Victor, and Tyler is eight."

"Nine," I say.

"Nine," he spits out in frustration. "If you think about it for a second, you'll realize how much you influence him. And it's stupid incidents like these that lead him down the wrong path."

That's actually pretty close to what I was thinking, but mine's a little different. I had considered ditching out on Tyler earlier back at school, and that's the only part about today I regret. I doubt Dad would believe the whole thing was Tyler's idea.

"And second," he goes on, "you took complete advantage of your sickness. It's not fair to yourself, and it's not fair to others that you think you can just have a free pass whenever you want and leave the rest of them in the dust. That's not how this works, Victor, and I really thought you would be mature enough to figure that out.

"And thirdly, you took advantage of your teacher. Your mother and I have met with Ms. Sherman many times, and she's been nothing short of generous in accommodating our situation since the beginning of the year. Were you aware of that?"

"No." I'm not sure I'm supposed to answer, but by then my face is buried so deep beneath my seatbelt strap that the words are muffled into more of a grunt. I push the seatbelt forward. "No, I'm sorry."

"Vic, you keep saying you're sorry."

"Well I *am* sorry!"

"But you're not learning from it! That's what sorry is—it means you'll never do it again. Now, you can keep saying

'Sorry, sorry, sorry' until your throat goes dry, but it doesn't mean a thing unless there are actions to back it up!" He slams his palm on the rim of the steering wheel.

I let the seatbelt snap back over my mouth—which I won't be needing—then I fold my arms together and look elsewhere.

The truth is that Dad's being unfair. He says I've been taking advantage of people—it's not like that. I'm only trying to help the world. I'm only trying to live like I know I need to. How can that be wrong?

"So what were you *really* up to today?" Dad finally asks.

I take a moment, deciding whether I really want to respond.

Dad continues. "Don't try to tell me you skipped class just to build your racecar. You could do that anytime. What were you really up to?"

"We went to the bank," I say, sounding more like a belch than a sentence. Dad raises his eyebrow.

"The bank?"

"Yeah, the bank."

"And what were you doing there?"

"Trying to open an account." I yank the seatbelt strap once more and continue pulling it out until it locks. "It's nothing," I say. "I wanted to make my own charity—you know, to help people. I don't even know why thought it would work, but Tyler said it would, so I went along to make him feel better. I'm sorr—er, I know it wasn't the right thing to do. I'll apologize to my teacher tomorrow."

Dad looks a little bit taken off guard. His face is screwed inward like he's thinking really hard, but I can't tell which part of what I said he's thinking over.

"You wanted to start a . . . a charity?" he says. The words are soft.

I ease into my response, like I'm peeking out to see if everything's okay. "Yeah. It felt right, I guess."

"How come?"

"Well, it came from the Dream Foundation. You know, we didn't have the best time, so I—we thought it would be nice to make one where it would actually help people make a difference instead of just trying to make them happy."

Dad pauses, thinks it over, and then continues with his nice voice. "So how did it go?"

"Not so well. We didn't really have any idea what we were doing. We were just stumbling over our plans, all unprepared and stuff. By the end of it, I could tell the lady was just being nice. Plus, you need to be an adult to open an account."

"So let me get this straight. You went to the bank and talked to the staff and tried to open an account for a charity all by yourself?"

"Tyler, too."

"Victor, that's impressive." He glances over my way just long enough for me to catch a twitch of a smirk, then he turns back to the road and adds, "But completely stupid."

I guess he can tell that I get the point. There's only so much you can yell at a person before they have to take over and live their own life. I hide my cheekbones with my left elbow in an effort to cover a smirk of my own.

"So you still gonna do it, then?" he says.

I look away. I hadn't thought about it since we got rejected. "I don't know. It was really hard, and Tyler and I don't know what we're doing."

Dad huffs. "Victor, in all this time trying to find a way to make a difference, did you ever think that that other people might want to do the same? You don't have to do everything on your own."

"I guess so."

"What if we got some people who knew what they were doing?"

"Like who?"

"Like your parents, for starters. We happen to have a lot of connections."

I think about it for a while. Before, I was afraid to ask them, I guess because I figured that they'd be afraid to help. But now here's Dad showing interest. For the first time in a while, it really seems like he's trying to help. I keep my eyes down. "Yeah. That sounds okay."

"Good," he says. "I can talk it over with your mother, and we'll see what we can do."

"Okay," I say, but then I add, "I would have to talk it over with Tyler first and make sure he's okay with it."

"That's probably a good idea. It seems like he's been really eager to be around you lately. Do you know why that is?"

I shrug. "I think he's just afraid, you know . . . of losing me."

"Well, when I came to talk to his dad, he seemed a little different than I remember him. I'm just a little worried that he's doing alright."

"I just think he's nervous. About me. About the racer. He wants it to be our project, so I don't think he wants anyone else involved."

"Are you sure about that?"

"Yeah, it makes sense, doesn't it?"

"I don't know. Just be sure to treat him well, that's all."

"I will."

We pull the car into our parking space, and Dad kills the engine. We sit there for a moment.

"You need anything else from me in the meantime?" He says.

I shake my head.

"Good," he says. Just before getting out of the car, though, he says one more thing, "Oh, and Victor? You're going to need to do a lot more than apologize to Ms. Sherman."

MATTHEW NEBEL

TIMEOUT

Seven Years Earlier

The tunnels Elijah White had been through before were all misleading. There was always supposed to be glory at the other end, but whenever he'd arrive, he would look for it, and there would only be a cold air that siphoned out any sense of achievement. The lights were all dim, and they all seemed to serve no purpose. Now Elijah stood at the edge of another tunnel. It was leading him away from the game he was born to play.

As soon as he'd broken the news about his retirement, the media was quick to prod at his reasoning. They asked why such an influential person as himself would give up his fame—the fame that allowed him to spread the word of God to people around the world. Elijah responded by saying that God never needed his help to spread the word.

"A football player is not who I am," Elijah once said. "A football player is my *job*. I don't know where the Lord will lead me now, but I know it will be somewhere great."

The next summer, during a warm-up drill in training camp, Gordon Fisher could actually feel that Elijah's bright, shining smile was missing. Without his mentor and friend, he felt empty and discouraged for the upcoming season.

He took a football in his hand, and tossed it downfield to a rookie wide receiver. But when the receiver caught the ball, he didn't give it to a coach. He turned right around and ran the ball back to Gordon.

What the hell is this kid doing? he thought.

The receiver handed him the ball, and stared at him. "You're Gordon Fisher."

Gordon hesitated. "Yeah . . . I am."

What was this kid wanting? An autograph? He was probably the fifteenth receiver on the roster, and only five would make the team. Maybe he was just trying to get anything he could before the final roster cuts.

"I just wanted you to know," the receiver said, "that I'm a hard worker, and a fierce competitor. I'll catch any ball you throw my way. That's a guarantee." Then, he smiled so wide that his teeth sparkled in the sun, and for a flickering moment, Elijah was standing right there beside him again.

There's something special about this kid, Gordon thought. He smiled back at the receiver. "Just keep catching my passes, and there will be plenty more to come."

He patted the man on the shoulder, and caught a glimpse of his name stitched onto the back. "Driver," he added.

"Sean," the receiver said. "Call me Sean."

4TH QUARTER:
KEEPING THE WHEELS TURNING

MATTHEW NEBEL

12

Starting a charity is a lot easier when you have someone else doing all the work.

After our talk, Dad started doing some research online and found a few sources that can help us out. He calls me into the kitchen that night where he's seated at the table with a ledger and a pair of reading glasses. To his left is Mom. But these days she's felt less like a mom and more like a relative you never actually see. It almost feels weird having her be a part of this conversation. But what else could we even do?

"The first part is the most important," Dad says. "We need to know what your goal is going be."

"That's easy," I say. "I want to help other people." Dad returns my hopeful look with one of confusion. "What?" I say.

"I just think we might want to be more specific. There are a million charities out there that all want to help people. What's going to make yours special?"

My face is clearly looking puzzled, because after a few moments Dad speaks up. "Why don't you think about the reason you wanted to do this in the first place? That could help get us going down the right path."

"Well, when I got to go to the Packer game through the Dream Foundation, it got me thinking a lot. I was excited, but it also felt kind of selfish, you know? I felt like I was taking. But I thought, if I don't have a real long life to live, shouldn't I be giving instead of taking?"

Dad hesitates, but I don't know if it's a good kind of hesitation.

"So," I say, "I want to help people live their dreams, but not the kind that happen to you—the kind that you make happen. The kind that make a difference in the world."

Dad smiles. "Did you come up with that?"

"Yeah, why?"

"Nothing. I just think it's very smart."

I get a warm feeling in my chest. I know he's not talking to his puppy. He really means it.

"So what do you want to do, then? How are you going to help people follow their dreams?"

And just like that, I feel a lot less smart. "I haven't thought about it," I say.

"Well, we can come back to that," Dad says, "but we'll need to have a clear direction if we're going to move much further."

"I've got an idea," Mom says. It's one of the first things she's said to me all week. Almost like she didn't know if she was allowed. "What if we made connections with other charity foundations, or even businesses, and we had them teach kids about success, and about helping the world?"

She looks to both of us, but I look to Dad.

"What do you think, kiddo?"

I nod. "I like it." I can see a flicker of a smile from Mom, but I still don't look at her all the way.

"Great," Dad says. "This is a great start, but we'll have to keep brainstorming if this idea is going to get off the ground."

I nod my head again. "I'll keep thinking about it," I say.

"Good." Dad looks down at the ledger once again. "Next, you'll need to free up your Friday. We have to head down to Madison to make it official with the state."

I nod my head, and Dad flips the ledger closed and asks, "Any more questions then?"

"Yeah," I say. "Tyler."

"Right. If Tyler and his parents give us permission and sign a few forms, his name will be on the paper."

"Great. I'll ask him what he thinks at school tomorrow."

But I don't catch Tyler when I get there in the morning. Granted I am a little late and a little anxious. I figure he's either in class already, or he's made a habit out of skipping school, in which case I'd be happy to know that I finally made a lasting difference in someone's life.

What I'm really worried about today, though, is what's waiting for me on the other side of the fifth grade door, because there's another task that I've been assigned.

I hear Jared's snarky voice first when I enter the room. "Hey Ramps, look who made it back."

"Stop calling me 'Ramps'!" Randy says as he stuffs a cold Pop-Tart into his mouth. "Hey Vic, what's up?"

"Hey guys." I throw my backpack down in the seat between them. "I'll be right back." As soon as I say that I begin to drown out their voices along with the buzzing of the entire room.

Ms. Sherman is at the front of the room wiping yesterday's lesson off the chalkboard. Looks like I'll never know what a conjunction is.

I cough once, and Ms. Sherman turns around. At this time I feel twenty-four pairs of eyes like ice on the back of my neck.

"Victor, glad to see you're back!" Ms. Sherman says. Those beaming eyes are like kryptonite.

"Ms. Sherman, I was wondering if you would like to join me and my family for dinner tonight." Oh God. Did I dream it, or did I really just puke those words up out loud? The room falls so quiet that I hear a Pop-Tart crumb fall from Randy's mouth and shatter on the floor.

She lays a hand on her cheek. "Tonight?"

I look around, waiting for someone to call "Dead man walking!" But when nothing happens, I reluctantly push forward. "Yeah—I mean, yes. Tonight. My parents were wondering . . . since I left early yesterday . . . you know I didn't really mean to . . . but I didn't tell the whole truth . . . so I guess that's why."

She looks at me and begins rubbing her cheek with her hand, apparently trying to figure me out. "Well . . . I am free tonight. What time?"

I sigh in my mind, knowing well that each word brings me closer to a permanent spot in playground horror story legend. "Six o'clock, if that works for you."

"Alright. That sounds great. I'll call your parents when class is over."

"Thank you." I hang my head, perhaps too early, and turn to walk the green mile back to my seat.

"It will be a pleasure to have her over," Mom said maybe forty times this morning. It wasn't a statement as much as it was a threat. In other words, "You'd better make it a pleasure, or else."

I take the long way home from school, hoping the extra wind might make my hair a little extra messy.

As soon as I get home, I check my hair in the glass panel of the screen door, and smile when I see that it's perfectly jumbled. I pry open the door, and let it snap back like a mousetrap once I get inside.

I find Mom and Dad are shuffling around, a lot like trapped mice. Mom almost clips me as I step into the living room, but she doesn't stop to say sorry. Dad is studying a page from a thin recipe book, fraying the pages apart with one thumb while the other grips a sizzling pan tightly on the stovetop.

"Hey Vic," he calls, as if the book in his hand were a script and he was just given the director's cue. "Why don't you go tidy up your room."

"Why?"

"We're having company tonight."

"Yeah, but she's not going to see my *room*."

"It doesn't matter. And we're having more than one guest. Go change your clothes while you're at it."

Mom rounds the corner, and the Victor Filter falls from her eyes. She looks at me and says, "Do what your father says."

"But—"

"NOW!" They both yell together, and I trudge down the hall to my bedroom.

There's a slip of paper on my desk. I snatch it up, and read the note—*Landon Burlington, Press-Gazette*—with a phone number beneath.

I walk out to the kitchen's entryway. "Dad," I say, "What's the deal with—"

"What?" The sizzling pan gets the best of his hearing.

I walk up to him. "This paper," I say, and hold it up to his face. I've got Mom's attention from the living room now.

"Oh, that," he says.

Mom butts in. "A guy from the paper called about doing a story on you."

"Why?"

"Well," Mom continues, "he heard about your trip to the game this week. He asked if he could spend some time interviewing you tonight. We thought it might be an opportunity to share your story."

"What makes you think I'd want to do that? I had a terrible time at the game!"

Dad eases softly into his words. "We know you did," he says.

"Well, then why did you do this?"

"Victor, first you need to stop with that attitude."

"But you're being rid—"

"Victor!" Mom scolds. "You will talk to us like an adult, or you will be disciplined like a kid."

I wish she meant it when she said that. I know some adult words I'd like to say to her right now.

"We know you didn't have fun," Dad says. "You've shown it in your eyes all week. The journalist, he wants to write about your time at the game. But I think you should talk about something else. Something you find more important."

And once again, I've completely underestimated my parents. The charity. A few thousand people read the newspaper every day; maybe it wouldn't hurt to get some more attention.

"Can Tyler come over then?" I say, skipping over the part where I admit they were right.

"Of course he can. Go call him up," Dad says.

"Wait," I say. "He wasn't at school today. I think he stayed home sick."

"Really?" he asks.

"Yeah."

Dad grinds his teeth together slowly. "Why don't you let me give his folks a call. We'll tell them what's up, and see if we can get him to come over."

But Tyler isn't able to come over, Dad tells me. He is sick, and he won't be out of the house for a few days. Part of me wants to reschedule the meeting altogether, but Dad tells me that this is the best night for it, because Ms. Sherman is coming as well. He knows her a little from the teachers' union, and says she could help with the charity—if we play our cards right.

The sun is setting earlier these days, and six o'clock is starting to feel more like eight o'clock.

The doorbell rings, though we don't even need a doorbell because the screen door is just as loud. Mom gets the door, and from my room I hear a swelling of happy-talk between her and Ms. Sherman.

"Why, hello there, Victor," Ms. Sherman says in a honeysuckle voice, as I emerge from the hallway.

"Hello," I respond. The grimace on Mom's face, which she's shielding from my teacher, lets me know that hello was not enough of an answer. "Welcome to our home," I add.

We offer to have her step into the living room and take a seat while Dad finishes setting the table and clearing the rest of the kitchen. Mom and Ms. Sherman stay in the living room talking about furniture until we sit down for dinner.

Landon shows up a little while after dinner. He looks a little like Hank from the Dream Foundation, trim with pointed smile, only Landon is a little bit older. I introduce myself, and shake his gorilla-sized hand. Then my parents and Ms.

Sherman introduce themselves, and we take a seat in the living room. Landon reaches in his bag and pulls out a small red spiral notebook and a little gadget that looks like a cheap iPod.

"Voice recorder," he says. He switches the gadget on and folds his hands.

"First, I'd like to thank you for letting me into your home tonight, Victor." He uses my name, but it feels more like he's talking to the recorder.

"No problem," I say. There's an unsettling vibe he gives off, and I can't put my finger on it. It's not like he's being overly snobby. For all I know, he may truly want to tell my story to the public.

He continues. "So . . . tell me. What's the prognosis from the doctors these days?"

Mom flinches, and I can tell Dad and Ms. Sherman are a little bit intimidated. It's a serious question, I know, but I've also been waiting for months to openly talk about my sickness. The honesty should be a welcome change. So then why am I still bothered?

Maybe it's me. My mind flashes back to Tyler, when he was clutching the racer plans tightly to his chest when his mom strolled into the room. He was trying to hide them, because they're his and not his mom's.

That's it. This is my story, and Landon is trying to turn it into his. I realize that if I want others to hear my story, I'm going to have to give up a part of me.

I look around the room, slow to finally speak. "Well . . . they say that I need a heart transplant soon. If I don't get an operation, I won't be able to live much longer."

"I see. So when is the operation?"

I shuffle in my seat. "There isn't one," I say.

Landon looks up, but he doesn't say a thing. I take it as a cue to keep on going.

"I can't get a donor—the waiting list is too long, which means that I probably have until around Christmas. Hopefully longer, but nobody really knows."

Landon looks like he's stepped into a minefield.

"Look," I say, "when I got diagnosed with cardiomyopathy, it was unlucky. But then I had someone famous notice me, and a lot of things started changing. I started getting attention. And I guess that was pretty lucky. But there are a lot of other kids out there who don't get so lucky. I don't want any of this attention to be the reason I get a transplant."

"Fair enough," he says. He starts to scratch some notes on the paper, then he looks up and pauses. "So, what are your feelings about that? Tell me what it's like knowing."

"It's easy for me," I say, "but I'll bet Santa's pretty nervous."

"Why's that?"

"Has to make me presents, knowing they're gonna be a waste."

The room falls silent. Landon obviously gets the joke, but he's not sure how to handle it.

"It's okay to laugh," I tell him. He lets out a grin, and Mom gives a sort of half, uneasy chuckle that people give when they're nervous.

"Do you believe in Santa?" He asks.

"No, I'm ten," I say, and Landon's grin widens.

I begin to feel more comfortable with Landon, which is weird. Maybe not knowing someone helps you be yourself with them. You're not so afraid of being judged. Maybe the world would be better if everyone acted the same way around the people they knew.

"Could I ask you a question?" I say.

He stops in the middle of a scribbling spree. Apparently I've taken him off-guard. Like a pro, though, he doesn't think twice about halting a dying boy's wishes. "Go ahead," he says.

"Do you think I look sick?" I ask.

"Well—er—"

"Be honest. It's okay."

"Honestly? You don't look sick at all. When I first saw you, I figured you were Victor's older brother."

"Thanks. That's what I keep telling people. I tell them I'm feeling fine, but they don't listen. They still treat me like I'm some kind of sick puppy who needs a belly rub or something."

Landon chuckles. "It's very important to be honest when you're speaking, but it's just as important to be honest when you're listening."

"That probably comes in handy when you're a reporter, doesn't it?"

"Well, nobody's perfect. I struggle more than you would think." His head goes back to the paper, and he jots down his longest note yet.

"So in light of honesty," he says, "I'd like to learn a little more about your time with the Dream Foundation. I hear you got to do some pretty neat stuff."

Then I realize that there are two different paths before me, and one would be harder to take than the other. I swallow a large gulp.

"With no disrespect," I say, "There's actually a different foundation I'd like to talk to you about."

Landon raises his eyebrows, but only for a second. When he sees the courage in my eyes, he responds, "Tell me about it."

So I do. I tell him my story of skipping school and going to the bank with Tyler. I tell him about getting caught, and admitting that I was only trying to do the right thing. And then I tell him what I think it means to do the right thing—to build strong relationships, and to be good to others. I tell him that that's what led to the idea for my foundation.

The whole time, I feel a little awkward spouting off my idea. But with everything I say, Landon responds with a smile that I can tell is true, and as time goes by, I begin to feel confident that my idea really is a good one.

Before Landon leaves for the night, he assures me, "You've got a good heart, Victor. You really do. It should be an easy task putting this story together." He smiles and turns to step out into the belting wind.

A little while later, Mom brings us more dessert from the kitchen. Ms. Sherman, Dad, and I keep talking.

"You know, Victor," Ms. Sherman says after swallowing a bite of her dessert, "I was thinking a lot as you were talking with Landon tonight. I figured that, if you wanted, I could talk with the rest of the faculty at school. I'm sure we could work out some sort of agreement with them to work with your charity idea. We already have plenty of connections with charities and businesses in the area. I'm sure many of them would love to hear about you, and even participate."

"We could even bring it up with the school district," Dad says.

I feel my face warm up, even though I'm almost certain that the ice cream I just swallowed was very, very cold.

"What are you planning on calling the charity, anyway?" Ms. Sherman says.

It takes me off guard. I haven't even thought about it. I look to Dad, but he doesn't have any idea.

But then Mom clears her throat. "I was thinking we could call it The Victory Foundation."

I hesitate, but when I run over the words in my mind, they seem to just click.

"Perfect," I say.

13

Friday morning, Mom, Dad, and I spend the whole day in Madison setting up the foundation. By Friday afternoon, everything is official, with me as the foundation's president, Tyler as the vice president, and my parents as the treasurers.

We get the name The Victory Foundation to the newspaper just before they start printing on Saturday night. And as soon as the paper starts hitting doormats on Sunday morning, I'm already receiving calls of congratulations from people I swear I've never even met.

Randy calls and asks if I could come sign autographs at his family's Packer game party. I kindly tell him I'll be watching the game with my parents. But that's a complete lie. After last week, the Packers are the last thing on my mind, so I won't be watching the game at all.

I'm still thinking about Tyler. He hasn't called me once since we both got grounded, so I figure he's either really sick or he's locked away somewhere.

I slip into class early on Monday morning, and I walk up to Ms. Sherman's desk.

"Hey Victor, I read your article," she smiles. "I thought it was phenomenal!" I actually blush a little when she says that.

"Thanks," I say. "I mean, it was good to see it and all."

"I'll say. Look here." She pulls a clipping of the article from her desk and shows me, as if I had been unaware. "I was thinking we could pass it around in class today. What do you think?"

"Umm . . ." What I really think is that I don't want to be pummeled with pointless questions for the second week in a row. On top of that, anyone who actually cares about the article's content would have already read it anyway.

"C'mon, Victor. It'll be great. You could stand up and tell them all about the experience."

I shuffle my feet on the floor. "Well, to tell you the truth, Ms. Sherman, I really don't want to." I say this in the most innocent voice I can muster.

She seems a bit heartbroken, but she says, "Not a problem. I understand."

It's a couple of minutes before Randy and Jared arrive and sit on either side of me. I pretend I watched the game yesterday and keep my mouth pretty quiet. I listen to them, and find out that the Packers beat the Washington Redskins—even though Gordon Fisher threw two more interceptions.

For most of the morning, though, I'm still thinking about Tyler. After class gets out, I'm headed straight for the third grade wing.

"Tyler!" I yell pretty loud. I scan the heads six inches below mine, but I quickly remember that Tyler's head would be even lower than theirs, so it feels a lot like a needle-in-a-haystack. The crowd starts to thin out and there's nobody left but a small group of girls and a scrawny little—

"Tyler?"

He looks bad. I look closer to make sure it's actually him, but there's no doubt. His skin is the color of cooking flour. In parts it looks blue, and his eyes are so sunken it looks like they're looking inward. Even his hair looks raspy and pale.

"Tyler, what's wrong?" He doesn't even look me in the eye. "Were you really sick? Are you . . . still sick?"

He doesn't really answer. He just gives a light shrug.

I don't know what to do, so I put my arm on his shoulder, but after only two seconds it starts to feel awkward, so I let it fall back to my side. "C'mon," I say, "I'll give you a ride home. We . . . we can work on the racer."

Then he speaks. I hear his voice for the first time in days. "Can we work on it at your house?" he says. But he doesn't sound like Tyler. He sounds like a five-year-old who just got over a time-out in the corner. I feel so bad for him that I wish there were another answer, even for such a simple question.

"Tyler, the racer's at your house."

"Oh . . . all right."

His eyes finally meet mine, but I don't recognize them.

We head out to the bike rack and kick off toward his house.

Tyler doesn't say anything when he hops off the bike. He only slides the door open with a loud lurch that makes my hair stand on end. Now there's silence.

Tyler goes over to the wall and pulls the hammer off its hanger. I yank the crinkled blueprints out of my backpack and throw them on the floor, then drag the racer skeleton to the center of the garage.

I pause. It hurts me, but I have to ask.

"Are you really okay Tyler?"

Tyler turns to me with the hammer in his hand. "Yeah," he says, and he just turns back and keeps on working.

Several minutes later the familiar BMW rolls up into the driveway.

"Hey, Victor, great article today!" Mike says as he shimmies his briefcase out of the car. Tyler quickly begins pounding a nail into a panel that he'd already finished a few minutes ago. His dad walks past and holds out a hand, and I slap him five. "I'll be in the basement most of the afternoon, but if you need anything you can come down and get me." He motions to the racer and says, "Lookin' good," before heading into the kitchen and closing the door.

Then Tyler loses interest in the nail and sets the hammer down on the floor. Now I can't handle it anymore.

"Tyler . . . what's wrong?"

"Nothing."

"Are you okay?"

"I'm fine!"

For minutes, then days, then years, we sit alone. We're not in the garage anymore; we're in a dark room, and there's nothing but me, Tyler, and the wooden racer skeleton lying on the empty floor between us.

"Tyler," I say, "what's wrong?"

He throws his head into his arms, and soaks the floor of the garage with his tears.

"No, no, no!" I scream, and leap from my feet, over the racer, and onto Tyler's body. I pin him to the floor and throw back his arms. His face is a deep red, like someone spilled wine into the flour, and his eyes are as sour as the grapes that made it.

"Tyler, what's wrong?"

"Nothing!"

"*What's wrong?*"

Then he shouts through his tears, "I don't want you to die!"

I let his arms fall limp, and he curls like a withering blade of grass. His short breaths shake his entire body.

I can't find the right words. I don't know if right words exist for now. I stay silent, but that doesn't feel right either. It just feels nothing.

"No one else likes me," he says, "None of the kids at school do . . . and . . . " he looks at the door, "and no one else does either." He sniffles a few times, and then he says, "If you die, I won't have anyone around anymore."

That hurts me. I wish I could just tell him it will all be all right. I can't though. Tyler is smart enough to see right through me.

"I don't want to work on the racer anymore," he says. "I've been thinking ever since we went to the game. I started thinking about the soapbox derby, and more and more, I realized it was a waste of time—for you, I mean. At first I wanted to keep going because it kept us together. But that was selfish. It's taking away from the time you could be spending making a difference. That's why I was so excited when you told me about your charity idea. I felt like it was a way to do both—to make a difference and keep you as my friend." Tyler pauses again. He's still shaking, but it also looks like he's thinking very hard. His eyes turn to the racer at his side. "The racer is meaningless."

I consider telling him that I don't know what to say or do. I consider telling him that I have been thinking a lot about meaning in life ever since the game too. I consider telling him that I've only recently discovered that everything in life is meaningless.

But instead I stand up, and I walk over to the pile of unused lumber. It's a lot smaller than it used to be, and I realize that we're not far from being finished.

I turn back to Tyler, who's now sitting up and looking at me, curious. He might be lonely when I'm gone, but right now I'm still here, and he still has a friend. I pick up a piece of plywood, bring it back to the center, and begin nailing it into the frame of the racer.

Tyler sniffles back a tear, and smiles.

When I get home, the light on the porch is flickering orange. A month ago, there would have been crickets chirping in the coming night, but now they've all gone to sleep for the fall, and everything is quiet.

I pass by Mom at the dinner table as she's filing through a stack of papers. She looks like I do when I'm doing homework, only a lot smarter.

"What are you doing?" I ask.

"Paperwork for the charity." At first I thought maybe she had gotten a new job, but doing paperwork for the charity is good too. "We got a few checks in today," she says.

"Really?"

"Yup."

"But how did we get them already if the mail doesn't go out on Sunday?"

She picks up one of the checks on the table and smiles. "People dropped them off at our door."

"Really?" I say. I stare gawk-eyed at the check in her hand. Scribbled in the first line is *The Victory Foundation* and just below it is *Twenty dollars*. On the table are others just like it, all with different amounts. I didn't even realize there was that much money to be had until now.

"All that came in just today?" I say.

But that's just the start of it. Once the checks start coming in the mail, there's more money than I ever knew existed. The kitchen table that was once used for utility bills is now covered only in checks and receipts. We eat all of our meals either at the kitchen counter or on TV trays in the living room. At the end of the table where I usually eat is a neat pile of thank you notes to the people who made donations. It's my job to seal them in an envelope and put them back in the mail.

On top of that, Dad says they've already found two charities willing to partner with ours. One of them pairs younger kids with older kids, like a role model, so the younger kids have someone to look up to. The other takes kids on field trips to visit businesses that do good in the community, so they can learn how to be successful and help others.

After only three days, the workload piles up so much that Mom decides she can't keep track of all the checks by herself. So she calls the school and negotiates to have them take care of the checks. Mom keeps handling the paperwork, and I keep licking the envelopes, but even those small jobs grow until we can't handle them ourselves.

The following Monday, Tyler comes over after school. By this time, The Victory Foundation has raised over six thousand dollars. When I tell him how well we're doing, he tells me that he needs to help out.

At the kitchen table that afternoon, he offers to take on the duty of envelope licking, but after a few minutes, his tongue is so dry that he can barely speak anymore.

"Are you sure you can keep it up?" I say.

"Yeah, ith no problemb," he says, "Path me another oned."

"Okay . . . do you at least want me to get you some water, though?"

"Water would be nithe."

We keep working along, and only after Tyler is a slip away from a paper cut on his tongue, Mom forces us to leave the table. But that's okay. We have some other work to do anyway.

Tyler chugs another glass of water, and a moment later, he and I are out the door riding my bike toward his house. We go a few minutes without saying anything, and the whole time I'm wondering what he's thinking. Is he even happy that he's helping?

Then he finally speaks up. "It's kind of weird," he says.

"What's weird?"

"Well, the racer has four wheels and holds only one person. Your bike has two wheels and holds two people. It's kinda the opposite."

"I guess so," I say.

"Yeah," he chuckles, "If you got a unicycle, you could fit your whole family."

14

Two weeks later, me, Tyler, and our families arrive at the racetrack, dragging along our racer on Tyler's trailer.

It's cloudy and windy, but the air outside feels fresh. The nearby lawns are covered with leaves, splattering the ground with patches of burnt red and yellow.

Our dads lift the racer carefully onto the pavement below while Tyler and I watch. The car is small between them. It almost looks like they're playing together with a Hot Wheels car.

The racer looks beautiful. We painted it dark green with a yellow stripe on both sides. Tyler wasn't sure if he wanted us to do Packer colors, but I made sure we did.

We did maybe a hundred practice runs in the past few days. Tyler learned to steer and brake like a professional. But standing there, watching our dads prep the racer, Tyler says plainly, "I don't want to do this."

"Yes, you do," I say. "You just don't know it yet."

I look around at the other kids that are gathered at the top of the hill. They're all small. Some of them are even smaller than Tyler. But Tyler's still shaking beside me, and I want to comfort him. That's when I remember the bag in my hand, and I hand it over to him.

"What's this?" he says, but without waiting for an answer, he starts unlacing the bag's handles that I tied into a knot. He pulls out a green piece of cloth that catches the small amount of sunlight.

"Your Packer jersey?" he says.

The smile on my face is wiped away. "You don't like it?" I say.

Tyler shrugs "Well, it's great, and all, but—" Then he stops, and folds it over his hand, revealing the name on the back in all capitals, and that's when it finally hits him.

"'*DRIVER*,'" he reads.

I smile. "Take us all the way, driver."

Behind the lip of the cockpit, Tyler is in a staring contest with the pavement ahead. The jersey on his back matches perfectly with the hull of the car, and together they make him appear as though he's peering over the canopy of a forest, like a predator ready to pounce on his prey.

I know Tyler is determined now that he's past the point of no return, but I don't want him to count his chickens too early. Five races separate us from the championship, and one loss will send the car back into the corner of Tyler's garage.

The kid in the car next to him looks determined too. His name is Phil, and he has long, scraggly hair that he has to brush out of his face every few seconds. Phil seems nice, but with all respect, I hope that he and his mom will be halfway home by the time Tyler is in the next race.

The rules to the race are clear and simple. Rule No. 1: When the referee drops the gate, the race is on. Rule No.2: The first one to the finish line gets to keeps racing. Rule No. 3: Don't blink, or you'll miss the whole thing.

The referee takes his stance beside the opening gate, which keeps the racers stalled at the top of the hill. He raises his hand to signal for the racers to ready themselves.

I can feel my heart crashing like thunder.

C'mon. Please, please let him win. He needs a win.

The hollow metal gate hinges downward and sputters onto the pavement, leaving only a small stretch of road in between Tyler and his finish line.

Immediately, the hard rubber cracks against the road. Both cars exit from the starting ramp, neck and neck. Tyler drops his head as low as he can. The belting of the wind whips him backward, but he holds onto the wheel and yanks himself forward, regaining control of himself and the car. Phil is not so lucky. He tries to swat the hair from his face, but it only flaps harder, hitting him in the eyes, and he struggles to keep his car straight.

When I realize that Tyler is going to win, I begin chasing the green *DRIVER* jersey the rest of the way to the finish line. God knows I could almost beat him there, I'm so happy. The judge at the finish line holds up his flag and points it to Tyler's racer. I throw up my hands in celebration, and I'm at Tyler's side before he can turn to see.

"You did it, buddy!"

Tyler has played it like a pro the whole morning. As happy as I've been, cheering him on, jumping around and violently shaking him in a big bear hug, he refuses to even make any hint of emotion. "We'll celebrate when we're in the winner's circle," he says.

He races a few more kids like Phil—and leaves each one in the dust. The last guy he races is significantly bigger than him, and that makes it all the more satisfying when the kid loses control and spins off the road, leaving Tyler with an easy victory. Whether there is a real winner's circle or not, I don't know. All I know is that Tyler is one win away from wherever it is the winner goes, because he's conquered everyone that has come before him, posting a perfect record of 4-0.

Now the wind pours in, and stings our faces. But most everyone sticks around for the final race.

Tyler will be racing against a kid named Max. He's one of the only people here that may just be smaller than Tyler. He races in a blue car with flames fading into white near the rear end. I'm a little nervous, but Tyler is as cool as ever. I see him walk over to Max and shake his hand while I check over the car. He eventually comes back over and stands next to me, but he's still staring down his competition.

"All set to go, buddy," I say.

Tyler looks down. "Thanks, Vic." He slaps me five and then I pat him on the back as he tightens the strap on his helmet.

"I know you're gonna do alright."

"Thanks."

"You know how I know?"

He looks at me as he struggles to fit the strap comfortably. "Hidden rocket engines?" he says.

I punch him lightly in the shoulder, and he winces. "No," I say.

"So what, then? Another Packer jersey? Someone with the last name 'Winner'?"

I smirk and pat him on the back. "No."

"How do you know, then?"

"Well . . . I guess I don't know."

"You want me to win," he says. He rubs his shoulder then finally locks his helmet strap in place and looks at me properly. Behind that stern face I can finally see Tyler and his charm. It's the kid I've been there for when he's been weak, and it's the kid that's been there for me all the time. I guess that's the reason I know he'll win. At least, he deserves to.

I walk back over to my parents, who each place a hand on one of my shoulders. The referee is settling in his place between them, and he asks each of the racers if they are ready. Max nods as if it has been his job his whole life, and Tyler gives the slightest tilt of his head before turning his attention to the familiar stretch of road ahead of him. The referee gives the ready signal. He puts his hand to the gate's lever. "Racers take your mark!" he shouts. "Get set!" He raises his arm.

My body starts to shake out of control.

The gate opens, and the two sets of front wheels immediately pour out of the starting ramp. Suddenly, it's a lot louder, as if I'd been unconscious this whole time. I hear the voices of my parents, and they cheer so loud that I shudder.

Tyler is flying down the road in a blur that smears the yellow and green paint on the side of the car together. Max is right beside him. My heart rises and shoves all the other organs out of its way, like it wants to peer over the crowd and see everything that's happening.

The two of them streak down the lanes. Green versus blue. The race is only seconds old, but it seems to take an eternity. I don't remember putting my feet in motion, but I realize that my shoulders have broken free from my parents' hands, and I'm chasing the two racers down the hill. Green and blue. Blue and green.

I trip and stumble to the ground. My hands fly out on instinct and absorb a part of the impact. My shoulder rolls over and collides into the dirt. Part of my cheek grazes the ground and scrapes my face. But I keep rolling, and soon I roll back onto my feet. I hear a cheer come roaring from the audience. My vision is blurry, with water seeping from my eyes. I take my sleeve and wipe it all away, and my vision comes back. I stare down to the bottom of the hill. The judge at the finish line holds up a flag and points to Max's car.

It doesn't seem right. It doesn't make sense. I think for a second that there must be some kind of appeal or re-race or something that would make what just happened not be true, but the only thing I can see is a swarm of people lining up to congratulate the young boy that isn't Tyler.

"Victor, are you alright?" I hear my parents run up from behind me.

I shove my parents away from me and run up to Tyler as he hops out of his racer. He takes off his helmet and sets it down in the seat, turning and watching the crowd that surrounds Max.

"Tyler," I say, but I can't think of anything else. We just stand there.

Then some older guy I don't know comes between us two. "Good race, boy. You did a great job," he says, and he gives Tyler a pat on the back before walking over to the circle of people in the other lane—the winner's circle.

"Tyler," I say again, "I'm sorry."

Tyler's face is stone.

"It's okay, Vic," he says. "There's always next year." He pauses after he says that. Then he looks away from me, and says nothing.

Our parents are around us a moment later, and everything after that is a blur.

Mom and Dad drag me to the reception lunch afterward. I don't think either Tyler or I want to be with those people right now, and it hurts even more that we're expected to nod and smile and get along with them.

"You've got some growing up to do if you think winning is the most important thing, mister," Mom says to me as we pull into the parking lot of a family restaurant. She adds the "mister" at the end to be all that more condescending. I keep my shoulders turned away from them, with my face staring out the window.

We get inside and the hostess greets us at the door.

"How many in the party today?"

"We're with the big group," Mom answers.

I scan the dark, musty room, and I'm surprised at how easily I can see Tyler. He's usually swallowed by anybody else that surrounds him, but now he's in between Max and Phil, who are on his same level. His parents are in the next booth over, chatting with some other parents. I take a step toward Tyler's table, and Mom taps me on the shoulder.

"Follow me this way," I hear the hostess say. She leads us over to a different table in a different section.

"See Victor?" Dad says. "You don't even have to sit by any of the other kids. Just us."

I look across the room and see if I can grab Tyler's attention, but he's talking to the other kids in his booth and he's waving his hands around, smiling, the same way he did the day that he told me about Heaven.

I don't talk to anyone on the ride home. I tread into my room and close the door. My eyes are still watering with grime from the sun and the cold weather and something else. I feel sick to my stomach and my head is throbbing like something's not quite right. I get down on my knees and bend over my bed, letting my face fall flat into my mattress.

I think about the piece of paper that's crinkled up and stuffed under my mattress, a few inches below me. I think of the entry I wrote just a few months ago, the one that says *Win the race with Tyler.* I'd rip it to shreds if it were in my hands right now.

I turn my head and look outside. It's starting to snow, and the sky is growing a dim gray that it does when the days become shorter. There's an eerie calm I feel when I try to track just one snowflake out of the thousands. I get up and go to my window, following one flake all the way to the ground where it melts onto a blade of grass. Sometimes I wonder if anyone else has ever considered a single snowflake. Millions come each year and some only live for a few moments. If you're a snowflake, chances are nobody will ever know you existed.

My leg starts shaking, and my head gets all fuzzy. The snow outside is no longer millions of tiny pieces of snow, but one single snow. White is everywhere. That's the only thing I can describe it as. And that's. That's.

Not right.

"Mom!"

I fall to the floor.

"Mom!"

The red and white lights are nothing to be afraid of. Mom tells me I have nothing to be afraid of. The nice people are just going to take me for a ride. I'm so confused and can't concentrate on anything, but that's what I think I remember Mom saying. Maybe it was a dream. Maybe I'm still dreaming.

15

They gave me a lot of blue medicine, and had me lie down and stay that way. They came with a tray that had a lot of weird food on it, and I told them I wasn't hungry. They told me it was good for me and I needed to eat. I tried one bite, but that was more than I needed, and they didn't ask me to eat after that.

I remember lying down with Dad sitting beside me, his face crusty with whiskers. I would fall asleep, then wake up, and he would still be there. I was sad because I wanted him to sleep, too. I wanted to take away my sleep hours and donate them to him, the same way that someone could donate an organ.

The days were as short as ever, but I didn't see the outdoors much anyway, so the nights all blended together, and it felt more like one long night that would never end. On what they told me was the third day, I received a giant poster board "get well" card from my classmates. They told me Ms. Sherman wanted to be the one to deliver it, but they wouldn't let people in who weren't in my family. Maybe that's why Tyler never came either.

Now I'm finally at home again. Mom and Dad are home too, and they're taking their shifts watching me. I feel weak and dizzy, like my head was hollowed out and filled with buzzing bees. When I go to the bathroom, I get really cold and shivery.

From the top of my bed with my head resting on the pillow, there isn't much of a view. From what I've seen, there's been a lot of white outside, which means the snow has come to stay. The past few winters in Green Bay have been pretty tame, but that usually means that the next one will be colder.

I curl the edge of my blanket up to my face to keep warm. The blanket smells stale, like it was soaked in a fish bowl overnight. It's been a while since Mom or Dad offered to wash it, but I don't bring it up.

I keep looking out the window as if there's any hope for me out in the bitter cold. Sometimes when the snow gets heavy, families will be stuck inside for more than a day at a time. I remember last year when the sun was blocked out by the weather for a week, and Mom started acting really weird. She got really sad for no reason, and she said it was the weather's fault. I'd never really understood that until now. It's worse because my friends haven't visited. Well, Tyler came once, but I was asleep, and my parents didn't want to wake me up.

I'm in bed for so long that Thanksgiving takes me by surprise. On Thanksgiving afternoon, during one of his shifts, Dad asks me if I want him to bring the TV into my room. The Packers are playing, and they still haven't lost a game since the game I went to. To everyone else it's a miracle, but to me it feels like a smack in the face.

I tell him that he can go into the living room, that I need my alone time. I still haven't left his or Mom's sight since I got home.

Dad eventually lets me be. Later he comes in telling me that the Packers won again. That makes ten wins, and still only one loss.

About a week later, I call Tyler to see if he can come visit. His voice is quiet, like he's trying to hide from something. He tells me he's busy and that he can't come over, but he'll get back to me soon.

On Wednesday, Jared calls me. But he tries not to talk about me, maybe to take my mind off of everything. Instead, he talks about the Packers. They're the only thing to talk about. They've got a game against the Cowboys coming up, and the Cowboys are the only team in the conference with a better record than the Packers.

"I made a bet on the game with Alex," Jared says. Alex is the only Cowboys fan in the whole school. Maybe the only one in the whole state, even. Jared goes on. "Whoever loses has to wear the same clothes every day for a whole month."

I chuckle a little bit and say, "Would that really change anything for you?"

The game is the next day, and Dad all but forces me to watch this time. He carries me out into the living room and sets me on the couch with my blanket.

"Come on," he says. "It's a huge game tonight. If we beat the Cowboys, that means we're in first place!"

I sigh. If only I cared.

Gordon Fisher lies back in the cabin of his horse-drawn carriage. There's an uneasy feeling in his stomach, and it's only worsened by the rumbling of the wheels over the rough dirt terrain below him. To his right is a small wooden chest. He's kept it by his side since the beginning of the journey, and he doesn't plan on leaving it until he's reached his destination. He caresses the handle.

Not much further, he thinks to himself, even though he knows that nothing could be further from the truth. He and his team are still in the middle of the Texas desert, and it could be days before they find themselves elsewhere. Out the window of his cabin, Gordon notices the curious way that the starlit sky touches the dry horizon, and he wonders which of the two is truly closer.

Then, a crippling scream comes from somewhere behind him. Gordon knows the voices of each of his teammates, and he knows that no one in his team could have made such a horrifying sound. A second later, he hears the deafening crack of a whip and perhaps a dozen sets of clomping hooves. He instantly grabs the small chest with both of his hands, and dares to peek his head further out the window. One by one, the carriages of his teammates are being trampled to the ground by a band of outlaws. He watches in horror as one of his good friends is wrestled out of his cabin door.

"Where is it?" the man yells to Gordon's friend. When he refuses to respond, he is only thrown to the ground like an afterthought. Gordon realizes that his protection is quickly dwindling, and the wooden chest starts slipping from his arms.

In a blur, a man on a horse passes by his window, and Gordon curls back into the cabin. A whip cracks again, and this time, it hits his own driver, who tumbles out of his seat and onto the ground. Gordon lets out a scream, but the noise is swallowed by the cranking of his carriage's wheels hard to the right. Gordon is thrown to the other side of the cabin from the momentum, but when he realizes that his carriage is still upright, he slowly climbs to his knees.

"Gordon!"

Somewhere, someone is calling his name, but he finds it hard to tell where, with his carriage now bounding quickly through the desert without a driver.

"Gordon!" the voice is closer this time.

Gordon jumps to the cabin window once again, and he sees the face of his friend, whose carriage is treading closely behind his own. Slowly, and dangerously, the carriage eases up beside Gordon's, and his friend reaches out his hands.

"Gordon, pass it here!"

Gordon shakes his head and clutches the chest closer. "I can't! It's too dangerous!"

His friend responds, "You've got to let it go!"

Gordon knows he's right, but he has trouble coming to terms with it. The chest was assigned to him. He knows that if his friend loses it, he and his team will be disowned.

Quickly, Gordon takes a new grip on the chest—this time from the bottom—and, reluctantly, he wedges it onto the windowsill.

"You'll have to get closer!" He yells to his friend.

The other carriage comes within a few feet of his own, and his friend reaches his arms out far. They're only inches away, but still not close enough to get a good grip. With one last lunge, Gordon shoves the chest fully out the window. His carriage hits a rock, and Gordon is thrown back to the floor. He grips his arm in pain, and turns his head to look out the window. To his amazement, the chest is still there. For a few glimmering moments it floats there, as though some miraculous force were guiding it to its destiny.

But it's not a miracle. A pair of thick, black gloves appears around the rims of the chest, swallowing it whole. It's an outlaw. Gordon tries to yell, but he cannot find the air. He's forced to watch as his entire life falls into the hands of the enemy.

Another crack of a whip tears through the air, and Gordon hears his horse release a helpless scream. His carriage starts to turn, and as it does, the outlaw pulls away from the window. Gordon is tossed to his side as the carriage tilts over itself. The horse lets out another cry and falls to the ground. Gordon crashes into the wall of his cabin, and shatters his right arm trying to brace for the landing. His body twists into a terrible shape and flings across the room as the wall becomes the ceiling and then becomes the floor.

Gordon clutches his right elbow. The pain tears at his body and encapsulates his mind.

A moment later, a medic clambers down to his side. "Gordon! What's wrong?" he asks, but Gordon doesn't respond. For all he cares, he's still completely alone.

"What happened?" Gordon shouts. "What happened to the ball?"

"They stole it," he replies.

"What?"

"It was intercepted, Gordon. C'mon, we need you to get off the field."

I cover my ears as Dad groans for the hundredth time tonight. He throws a pillow to the floor and comes close to letting out a swear word.

I'm different, though. I almost flicker a smile as I watch Gordon walk into the locker room clutching his right arm. A few seconds later, the camera pans back to the field, and the Cowboys score another touchdown.

"Oh, this is just perfect," Dad says. "Just what we need when we're down three scores—now Gordon's leaving the game."

Dad ends up leaving the game early, too. I stay on the couch and watch the backup quarterback struggle to take over the reins. In the end, though, even he plays better than Gordon. He brings the team back to within three points, but they run out of time, and they lose their second game of the season. I'm starting to think it's bad luck for me to watch the games.

With Dad mumbling in the kitchen, I turn off the TV and drag my blanket back to my bedroom. I close the door, and lie back on the mattress.

16

I think of Tyler a lot over the next few weeks. He still only visited me that one time, which was almost a month ago now. I figure even a phone call would be nice, and it used to be that he was able to get from his house to mine faster than he could even dial the numbers.

He hasn't even helped in The Victory Foundation. When Ms. Sherman came over for a visit last week, she said she hasn't seen him at any of the meetings she's been holding after school.

The foundation could use his help, too. According to Ms. Sherman, she hasn't seen much of anyone at the meetings, and because of that, she says that very little has gotten done so far. She seemed sad. When I saw her sunken face, I wished that I could go help.

But I'm not even allowed to leave. My room is like a prison. Even the walls feel colder than the air they try to keep me sheltered from. And I feel empty.

I take a tissue from the box at the side of my bed and blow a huge gob of boogers out of my nose. If I wasn't empty before, getting rid of that snot rocket did the trick.

BAM!

I jolt in my bed. My first thought is that a bird must have flown into my window. But it's nighttime, which means birds aren't out flying. And it's winter, which means birds aren't anywhere right now. I look at my window. A large chunk of snow is spread across the top panel.

BAM!

And another. I jump out of bed. My legs are weak, and it's been so long since I've risen that I've forgotten where the squeaky floorboards are, and how squeaky they are. I steady

155

myself on the window frame and peer outside. The face that looks back is buried under a wool scarf and a winter hat, but the eyes sparkle through the darkness. It's a sparkle that I know by heart.

"Tyler!" I press my hands to the glass, which freezes my fingertips and makes my arms shiver. The clock on my desk reads 12:41.

I latch open the locks on the panel and shimmy the bottom upward. A gust of snowflakes blows into my room, and the air howls through the crack below my bedroom door.

"Tyler?" I whisper. Tyler inches closer to the window, his rubber boots squeaking over the wet snow as he steps. The top of his head reaches to about six inches below the windowsill, so he has to get on his tiptoes, pull himself higher with his hands and crane his neck to get closer to my level.

"Can you come play?" he asks.

"Tyler, what're you doing here?"

"I'll show you. Just throw on your winter stuff and meet me outside." He treads around the corner, leaving nothing for me to look at but his footprints in the snow.

The hallway is dark, so I grab whatever gear I can find from the closet, whether it's mine or not. I sweep it all into my arms and peer over the pile as I make my way to the back door.

Tyler is waiting outside. The pale orange glow from a street lamp is shining over the thick snow on the ground, and it glints off every heavy flake that falls from the sky. The first breath I take reminds me of how stale the air is inside. I feel like my lungs are being shaken out like a rug. I struggle to lace one of my boots. "So what did you need?" I say.

"I got you a Christmas present," he says.

"Couldn't it have waited until *Christmas*, then?"

"Well, it's past midnight, so technically it *is* Christmas."

I stop. Could it really be Christmas already? It doesn't seem like it. I haven't seen any tree or decorations up in the apartment, but that could be for other reasons.

Tyler beckons me to follow him with his small blue mitten. I get up and try to steady myself. "You gonna be okay?" he asks, and I nod. My legs are still wobbling, and the added pounds of my snow clothes make it harder than I hoped, but I know I can make it on my own.

He leads me to a park with a large hill. Half of it is covered with forest, and the other half is bare. At his signal, we start trudging up the edge of the tree line. With each step, the snow reaches the bottoms of my knees and nearly swallows Tyler whole. A quarter of the way up I fall forward.

"Vic! You okay, Vic?" Tyler rushes to my side, but I brush him away.

"Yeah, I'm fine. Just a lot of walking." He grabs my arm and helps me back to my feet.

"We can go back," he says.

It's a tempting offer. My toes are freezing, and the frigid air is whipping at my face, turning my lungs into stone. But Tyler has something big planned, I can tell. Otherwise he wouldn't have dragged his sick friend out of bed at midnight in a blizzard.

I hug my jacket close to my body, trying to seal the gap between the neckline and my collarbone. I squint through the mammoth snowflakes battering at my face. Just inside the tree line I can see the outline of something big and bulky.

"Tyler?" I pant.

He turns, and several flakes of snow find their way onto his eyelashes. He rubs them away, and puts his hand up like a visor.

"What are we doing here?"

"Take a look around. Take in the atmosphere."

I shoot him a skeptical look. When his face doesn't change, I decide I should take him seriously.

I turn and look down the hill, over everything in the park, over half the neighborhood—well, what I can see through the snow, anyway. I can't see any houses in any direction for a few hundred yards. It feels a little bit surreal up here. Really calm and blank and white. I close my eyes and try to block everything out. Then . . .

THUNK!

My left knee buckles, and I let out a huge cry of pain.

"Vic, I'm sorry, I didn't mean to—!" Tyler's voice ends with a struggle. I've fallen face down into the snow. It's a fight trying to turn over, but I turn my waist just enough to face Tyler.

"What was that?" I ask, with half my vision still blinded by the snow covering my face. I see Tyler grunting and struggling to tug something back up the hill. It must be the object that was in the forest.

"Tyler?" I yell. I hear a few more grunts come from his direction.

"Vic?" He says.

"Yeah?"

"Have you gotten any lighter since you've been sick?"

"Yeah, like ten pounds."

"You feel like running?"

"No."

"Too bad." He lets out a yell of pain as he lets the object go. The next second I feel a pair of hands slide beneath my arms and hoist me up. "RUN!" He yells. He pulls me with him, and we both go booking it down the hill.

I'm out of breath after just five steps, but the urgency in Tyler's voice is enough to give me the strength for an extra six or seven. I swat the remaining snow out of my face, and only then does it become clear what we're chasing. The racer.

Tyler is quick as lightning, and I'm going as fast as I can, but I'm struggling to suck in air and his boots are kicking up clumps of snow in my face with every stride. I see him finally catch up to the car and whip his leg over the side wall. A second later he's kneeling inside, turned around and waving me forward.

"COME ON!" He yells, plummeting further and further down the hill. As I chase after Tyler and the car, I feel like I'm back at the raceway chasing his car down the lane in the championship round. My legs feel like they're deflated, but I don't want to let him slip away from me this time.

Tyler stretches out his hand, but I'm at least a dozen feet away. The car hits a bump and sends Tyler up and back down into the seat. But the car slows down. I take my chance. I leap through the air and land on the rear end of the car. Tyler's hands land on my own and he struggles to pull me upward. My boots are dragging through the thick snow, but the car doesn't even think to slow down. We've hit the steepest part of the hill. The point of no return.

BAM!

We hit another bump, and I slide a few inches forward.

"C'mon! You've got to pull!" He yells. I pull and he pulls, and I slide further up the car. With one great lunge, I'm yanked into the car's tiny cabin.

"Sit up!"

"I'm trying! I'm trying!" I gather my balance and slip into the only chair. "How is this thing rolling through the snow?" I shout.

But Tyler is fidgeting his legs in front of me, trying to find a way to face forward. The car is picking up speed, and I have no idea where we are on the hill or what lies ahead of us. I slide myself as far back as I can into the seat, and he barely squeezes in between me and the front of the car.

"There!" he yells in triumph. He turns around as far as he can. "You comfy?"

I nod my head yes, but when I do, I see something that's not so comfy. Just ahead of us is a large oak tree.

"Tyler, turn left!" I point in front of us. He quickly turns his head and I can no longer see his eyes, though I'm sure they're the same as my own. "Tyler! Left!"

That's the last thing that happens before I see the world upside down. It's the first time tonight that I'm thankful for the snow. I thump to the ground. To my right, I hear gasping, which means Tyler is still breathing.

"Tyler?"

". . . Skis . . ." he huffs.

"What?"

" . . . Skis . . . I replaced the wheels . . . "

"Wait . . . really?"

" . . . Took me a month to get it right . . . "

Then we just lie there panting. My jacket is soaked in a warm sweat; the cold air is actually feeling pretty good now.

The only damage was a few scrapes across the front. Tyler doesn't even let me help tow the racer back. He insists he can tug it the whole way home.

"I dragged it all the way here, didn't I? And that was up the hill, too."

We keep walking through the silent night, our boots squeaking against the packed-down snow in the street. Every once in a while, we have to swerve out of the way of a street lamp so no one sees us and calls the cops. The snow keeps falling and our eyes stay squinted thin. Once we get to the corner where he and I branch off, we stop for a minute. Tyler hops onto the front of the car and takes a breather, and we both take in the scene.

"Hey Tyler," I say, neither of us looking at each other. "You remember when you told me what you thought Heaven was like?"

"Yeah."

"That's what it felt like on the top of that hill."

"I don't think I mentioned getting clipped in the leg."

"Not that part. The scenery. It was just kind of weird, and peaceful."

"Yeah."

I think for a moment. Then I say one more thing. "You hadn't talked to me in a month, Tyler."

He looks down. "Yeah, I know Vic. I'm sorry." He slams his fist on the racer. "I was just trying to get this piece of—"

"No, that's not what I mean. You hadn't talked to me in a month, but you kept on building. How did you know I'd be healthy enough to come out here with you?"

"I don't know," he says. "I guess I didn't know if you'd be healthy or not. I didn't really think about it."

Back outside my apartment, the yellow porch light is flickering disapproval in my face. I don't like its attitude, so I trudge around back. Once I get around the corner of the house, I notice that the light is on in my kitchen. The faint smell of coffee wafts into my nose when I pry open the back door.

Mom and Dad are leaned against opposite counters. As soon as I step in, Mom's arms latch around my shoulders.

"Thank God you're safe!" She swivels me from side to side, then pulls herself back and takes a wider look at me. "Where the hell have you been?" Within seconds, she's bawling over me, and her tears are melting the snowflakes on my jacket.

"I was out for a walk."

"That's funny," Dad says wiggling the phone in his hands, "cause apparently Tyler is out for a walk right now."

I'm not fazed at all. I know that I'm sick, and I know that I should be in bed, and I know that I should tell them when I'm leaving the house for the first time in weeks. I also know that I just had more fun than anyone could ever take away.

"Victor," Mom says.

"What?" I scowl, maybe a little bit more sharply than I needed to. Then for a rare moment, I look into her eyes. They're soft and reflective.

"We're just glad you're home," she says, and her voice warms the room.

"You mean you guys aren't mad?" I say.

"You're grounded forever," Dad says, "but we are glad that you're home. Now let's get to bed. We'll talk in the morning."

"Thanks," I say, and I trudge off into the hallway.

Before going into my room, I turn and see a few crudely wrapped boxes on the living room floor. I realize they probably got up to put out the presents and noticed that my door was open.

I step inside my room, close the door and lie down on my bed. The snow is still pelting the ground outside, but all is calm in here. I notice the clock reads 2:35. That means we were out there in the cold for almost two hours, and it definitely *is* Christmas morning. I close my eyes. The bees in my head finally decide to drift away to sleep, and I do the same.

At 3:05, my eyes jerk open. I thought I dreamt it, but maybe it was real.

"Victor!"

It's definitely real now. I roll over and rub my eyes. Before I can open them back up, the door is open, and Dad is standing in the frame.

His voice is demanding. "Victor, come to the living room right now. We need to talk to you."

What's going on? Did they change their minds that fast?

I let out a yawn like a lion. "Dad, I'm tired."

"This can't wait, Victor. Something's happened, and we need to talk to you right now."

17

I wrestle my way out of bed. Mom and Dad are both waiting for me, and Mom is sipping on a cup of coffee I'm guessing is still from the same pot they made earlier. Mom looks worried. Dad looks serious.

"What's wrong?" I ask.

"Can you please sit down?" Dad says, pointing to the chair next to him. A lump forms in my throat, but I don't know why it's there. I sit down on the green sofa and tuck my legs into a pretzel.

"Victor, we just got off the phone with Tyler's mother." When he says this, Mom starts crying, little hints of tears welling on her face. Without warning my own body starts pouring out water as well, but mine is a hot, nervous sweat. Dad looks like he could join either of us at any moment, but he keeps his head level as if it were his only hope. "We had talked to both her and Tyler's father earlier tonight when you two were out missing, and again when you each got home."

"I'm sorry Dad," I say right away. I am sorry, but I have no idea what for. I'm sorry for ever hurting them or ever possibly hurting anyone. Now the tears begin to form, and I dip my head down into my knees.

He puts a hand on my shoulder. "Victor, nothing you did was wrong. You've been the best boy in the world. And you've been the best friend in the world to Tyler, too, and that's what matters most."

My heart swells. "What happened? Is Tyler okay?"

Dad shuffles. "No," he says. "He was hurt tonight."

"How?"

"That's not important right now, Victor. He and his mother are on their way over here, and they're going to be staying with us for a while. So we need you to keep on being a good friend to him, like you always have, okay?"

I don't answer. I just press him further. "Why are they coming over? What about his dad? Where's he gonna be?"

Dad closes his mouth. It looks like he's out of words to say, like they've just emptied out of his mouth and there aren't any more left.

Mom has me go into my room and crawl into bed. After a few minutes, she brings in a small rollout mattress and throws a twin-size sheet over the top. She doesn't even speak to me. When she's halfway out of the room, I half-yell. "Mom!"

She peaks her head back through the door. The light from the hallway has her silhouetted like an angel. "Could you come here?" I say.

She walks quietly across the floor, as if she's lighter than the creaks in the floorboards. She sits down on the edge of my bed and looks into me. I look back into her, and the softness of her eyes break me. "What's the matter?" she asks.

"I—" The words can't come out, because my mouth no longer belongs to me. It belongs to the tears welling in my eyes. I bend my head down and let the tears spill out into the world.

I feel her hand on my back. "Victor, honey, what's that matter?"

"I don't want you to feel bad anymore," I sob the words between my hands.

"What do you mean? I don't feel bad. None of us did anything wrong."

"No, I don't mean with Tyler. I mean with me. I've been mean to you ever since that night I came back from the game," I say. When I say it, I know she remembers. She keeps rubbing my back, but there's a little shake in her hand. "It was 'cause you didn't answer me," I say. "I was looking for an answer, and you just kind of left."

"I know," she says.

"Then why'd you leave?" I look up, and I see her cheeks and forehead are red, and I can only imagine that my own face looks the same way.

"I'm sorry, Victor. I'm sorry."

"I needed you."

"I know, Victor. I know. Come here." She prods me into her arms and I give her a hug. Both of our clothes become soaked in each other's tears. She keeps crying, but keeps speaking too. "It was like your dad said, Victor. We were all scared. I was so scared that I didn't even realize that that's what it was. And then you brought it up. You threw it out into the open, but I just wasn't ready. I was scared to tell you the truth—that I was scared."

"I'm sorry!" I say loudly into her shoulder. "I never wanted you to be sad. I never wanted to do anything wrong."

"No, no, you don't have to be sorry. You did *nothing* wrong, Victor. You did everything right. I was wrong. I'm so sorry."

"I just want everything to be okay!"

"Me too, Victor. I want us to be happy." Then her voice becomes soft and tender. "I want you to be happy."

She brings me into a tighter hug and keeps her hand to my back, like she's guarding a small baby from the wind.

"Mom?"

"Yes?"

"I need you to be honest with me, then."

"I will."

"Promise?"

"I promise. I'm just scared. That's the truth. I just . . . I just don't want you to be scared. I don't want to see you scared . . . I tried to get away from it all. It was selfish. I'm sorry."

I sniff back a tear. My lungs take in a quick gasp of air, and hers do the same, as if our breaths are tied together. I pull back from her, and I look into her exhausted red eyes again.

"Okay," I say. "I forgive you."

In some time, I tell Mom that it's okay for her to leave the room again—that I need to be alone.

I look down at the mattress that's supposed to be for Tyler. It frays at the edges, and some of the seams are torn apart. Its corners all curl upward like it's gasping for air. I look at my own bed. It could be on its last breath, too, but it's still better than what Tyler is getting. I wish I could give him my bed, but I don't think Mom or Dad or Tyler would let me.

The screen door screeches, and I dig my head underneath my blanket for some reason that I don't know.

I hear mumbles in the entryway. Soft, disturbed mumbles between two women. My stomach starts to churn. When is Tyler gonna come in? Will it be in a few minutes? A few hours? A few seconds? I want it to be over.

My door cracks open. The hinge squeaks so loudly I have no excuse to still be asleep. I curl the tips of my fingers over the top of my blanket and peel it down below my eyes. Tyler is there, alone. The only light comes from the moon through the window, dampened by the snowballs that Tyler had thrown just a few hours ago.

"Tyler." My voice is muffled by my blanket, but I stay hidden beneath it.

He doesn't look interested in what I have to say. He just looks at the mattress on the floor and walks over to lie down on it. For a moment, the moonlight flickers onto his face. It's the first time in a month I've seen his whole face, not covered by scarves and hats. It's white like a ghost, but his left cheek is a puffy dark rainbow, with only red, purple and blue, and it covers most of his eye.

He lies down and curls over to face away from me. I watch him for a moment, and turn back over in my bed, hugging the blanket tightly to my chest.

In the morning, Dad tells me that he, Mom and Tyler's mom have some things to take care of out of the house. He wants me to stay here with Tyler and keep an eye on him. But Tyler is still asleep, so I go out into the front hall.

On the kitchen table, I spot a tall stack of card paper. I pick one off the top. It reads *Happy Holidays* on the front. On the back is a small note in Mom's handwriting, addressed to some random person. It says:

> *Season's Greetings from The Victory Foundation. We wish you a happy and healthy holiday with your loved ones, and we thank you for your continued support. Every donation, however big or small, helps us to change the world one life at a time.*

I feel guilty. I haven't been able to go to any of the meetings. Everyone has told me that I need to stay home and rest, and, well, I guess I just went along and believed them. But last night, on that hill, I think I proved that I'm strong enough to do anything.

I put the card back on the table with the rest of them. Mom has been working hard. I just want it to be worth it for her. I don't want the foundation to fizzle out. I want to help. I want Mom and Dad and especially Tyler to finally get something good.

I go out to the living room. On the floor, I notice the small pile of presents still waiting to be opened. I nudge a few boxes around with my feet. Some are from distant family whose only communication with us is through Christmas presents.

One of them isn't even wrapped. It's a football with signatures all over it. The tag on the side says:

> *Dear Victor,*
> *Thanks for visiting us earlier this year. We wish you and your family a blessed holiday season.*
> *—The Packers*

I roll it around by the two points and examine all the names. There's Sean's, I recognize from my hat. Gordon's is the biggest of all, and he wrote out his full name instead of just a few little scribbles.

I push the rest of my presents off to the side so that Tyler might not notice them as much when he gets up.

In the late evening we're seated around the kitchen table with the dusty old Scrabble board at the center. We managed to get Tyler out of bed to play, but he didn't want any dinner and he still isn't talking. I guess that's okay right now. You don't really need to talk in Scrabble anyway. Just let the letters do the talking.

While Tyler's mom thinks over her next move, I draw a tissue out of the box at my side and blow out some snot. The buzzing is back in my head tonight, and I'm still exhausted. It kind of makes it hard to concentrate, but I do my best to put on a good face for Tyler's sake.

I look at my tray and ponder the seven letters before me: *YIEKREA.*

What can I do with that? I start fidgeting with a few of the tiles. Maybe I could make something with *YAK* or . . . something with *REA.* But nothing looks open from what I can tell. I hear someone sigh, but I'm too focused to tell where it came from. With one swipe I pick up two tiles and throw them around the *G* in someone else's word, *STRENGTH.*

"There." I say. "*AGE.*" Not quite worthy of the Scrabble hall of fame. "Let's see, that's worth . . . four points. Oh, wait, that's a double word score, so eight."

"Beautiful," says Dad, and I shoot him a nasty look. I yank another tissue from the box and blow more snot. Then I reach to the letter bag to draw two more tiles.

"Victor! Wash your hands first, please!" Mom scolds. I stop my hand inches from the bag and head to the sink to get some soap.

"I'll get your letters for you," Tyler's mom says. "I won't look at them, I promise."

It's Tyler's turn next, and he's already twiddling some of the letters around in his fingers, looking thoughtful. I figure that's either because he truly is thinking, or just because the letter tray gives him somewhere to look that isn't at any of us. I get back to the table and wait for him to move. After a few moments, he scrapes off four letters and thumps them down behind *AGE*.

COURAGE.

We all give him a round of applause, and a trickle of a smile breaks free from the corner of his mouth as he looks into our eyes for the first time. Just that little bit of happiness could be enough to power the whimpering light bulb above us. It's not much, but it's a start.

As we're laughing and cheering, I take a moment to look around at the four other people seated here. Then I look down at the table. The table is old. It wobbles every time someone lays down an elbow or picks up a glass of milk. But it's still a table. It was meant for people to sit at so they could look at each other. Maybe the things we own aren't in the best shape, and maybe we don't have the most money in the world right now. But once we're seated together, it becomes surreal, like there's a ring around this table and the people seated at it, and nothing outside the ring matters at all.

I don't know if it's just my mind playing tricks, but the light bulb above me seems to brighten up. The whole room does, actually. The whole room is vibrant, and the people and the laughter and sight and sound and touch and taste and smell and life all blend together and now the room is glowing. I grab the table. It vibrates and shakes everything I know inside and out, all the way up into my brain. I look up again. The light bulb is so, so, *so* bright. Now, I'm looking at it from the floor.

Someone far off in the distance screams my name.

But I'm falling, and they'll never reach me.

MATTHEW NEBEL

TIMEOUT

Three Years Earlier

Elijah White fell asleep on Christmas night. During that night, God took him into a warm embrace and brought him away. He was young. He was healthy. And yet, it was still his time.

Sometimes it's hard to understand why God does things like this. A man like Elijah was one of His most faithful soldiers, and he was taken from the battlefield so early in his life. Elijah's work on Earth is done, but his fingerprint will continue to make a difference in the lives of those he's left behind.

But God did not intend to put Elijah to rest just yet. He intended to use Elijah for a different purpose. And his next assignment will be the most important of them all.

At every turning point in his life, Elijah had found himself running down a tunnel in search of glory. Now, he stands at the edge of a new tunnel. He's finally found out what true glory means, and he's ready to take the hands of others and lead them down the path.

MATTHEW NEBEL

OVERTIME:
TROUGH THE SNOW AND RAIN

MATTHEW NEBEL

18

Victor can't talk all that much anymore, and he's stuck in bed now. When he went into the hospital, he was blue. People talk about feeling blue when they're sad, but I didn't know someone could actually turn blue.

They asked me if I wanted to be with him on the way to the emergency room, and I said yes. I felt strength and courage to be with him, but when I saw him, I lost it all.

I remember Mom telling me to wait in the waiting room, but I couldn't stand it in there either. The walls were blue too, and all I could think of was why do they make rooms like this, where people go to be sad with each other. I ran outside where the snow was falling. I wanted it to block everything else out, and be like Heaven, like Victor said. But the world was still there, and it wasn't leaving. I fell down and cried so hard that I couldn't make any tears.

I never meant to let him down at all. I want to tell him how much he means to me.

I think back to the night in the Packers locker room. I remember how my legs trembled when the man started yelling. I've heard a lot of men yelling lately. But that night, Victor stood up and showed me that big yelling men aren't as powerful as they want us to think.

Victor doesn't know this, but that's what helped me finally stand up to Dad when he did more than just yell—the night he found out I snuck out with the racer.

That wasn't the only time, either. Vic always tried to convince me that I was braver than he was. He helped me be brave at the race, and he even helped me make new friends.

But now I don't feel brave at all. That night in the hospital, Victor proved that he was always the brave one.

Now he's back home, but he's in rough shape. We have to be by his side every second of every day, which has gotten a lot harder ever since the holidays ended. I have to go to school, even though I'd stay here every second if I could.

On a Saturday night, I bring a bowl of soup into his room. The only light comes from this dim little lamp we brought in so we could see while Victor was trying to sleep.

"Hey Vic. You don't have to eat it if you don't want to. My mom just thought it'd be nice."

He makes a light gurgling sound, which I take to mean that it's fine. He presses his face close to the rim of the bowl and starts ladling some of the broth into his mouth.

"The Packers won," I say. I know he doesn't care, but I'm willing to try anything to lift his spirits a little. He just keeps sloshing his soup, and I'm not really sure if he's paying attention or not, but I guess it's good that he's eating, so I keep on talking.

"We beat the Seahawks. It was actually a pretty good game. We went down fourteen-to-nothing right away. But then we started cooking, and Gordon—well, we scored like forty straight points."

"I could hear the yells," Victor's voice is like a rusty car.

"You could? Well, sorry, we'll try to keep it down next time—"

"No." He says, and he looks out the window. The snow is billowing to the ground—the same snow that billowed down on Lambeau Field in a blizzard earlier tonight. I realize he means he heard the yells from the stadium a few blocks away.

"Is the season over now?" he asks.

"No, it's not over. It's the playoffs."

"Mm," He drops his spoon in the half-empty dish and slinks further into his bed, then casually says, "Maybe I'll watch next time."

"I'd like that," I say.

It's hard to see him like this, exhausted from eating half a bowl of soup. I feel like I would trade places with him in an instant, just so I wouldn't have to look at him, but I doubt I could stand what he's been through.

"How's the charity doing?" he asks me. But I don't know if I want to answer.

"Not so well," I say.

"Mm," he groans one more time, and turns over the other way.

It's the middle of January now. Victor keeps getting sicker, and the winter isn't showing any bright days ahead. Sometimes I just try to keep my mind on other things, and having the Packers helps.

A lot of people who aren't from here don't really understand why football means so much to us in the first place. But I think the winter has a lot to do with it. In Wisconsin, it can get so cold that it hurts, and even makes you sad. But the Packers bring people into the living room and squeeze them together on the couch so they can make each other warm.

As long as the Packers are still playing, the cold doesn't seem so bad.

After school on Wednesday, Mom takes me over to Max's house so we can let Vic have some time alone with his family. I think Mom is eager to get out of the apartment for a while. She's felt bad ever since we moved in, like we owe them now for staying there.

But I wish I could stay with Vic. Everything reminds me of him anyway. Like Max. If Victor didn't push me to be brave and drive in the soap box derby, I never would have even met him in the first place.

I walk down into Max's basement and leave both of our moms in the kitchen. Max is sprawled out across the floor along with a giant pile of Legos. I see him snap two bricks together and then look up to see me in the middle of the staircase.

"Hey, Tyler! C'mon down." He waves me over with his free hand, and I go to join him on the floor. We start raking our hands through the pile, scattering the pieces everywhere and sending a shattering echo off the concrete walls.

"How've you been?" he asks. "You look like you just had a close encounter with a bug zapper."

I smile, but it's a fake one. "I'm okay," I say. I figure I don't want to talk about Victor with Max today. Not because he wouldn't care, but because he wouldn't really understand. So, like everyone else these days, I talk about the Packers.

"Did you see the game the other night?" I ask.

"Yeah, of course. Gordon's looking pretty good. They keep talking about how he'll probably retire after the season."

I manage to laugh. People have been saying that every year since I've been alive. Last week, I was in the living room when that discussion came on ESPN. Victor's dad groaned in his armchair. He quickly turned off the TV and said, "I'm done. I just don't care anymore," and got up and walked away, and I chuckled quietly to myself.

"Do you think he'll retire?" Max says. The image of Gordon flashes in my mind, angry and yelling.

"Well," I say, "that time I got to meet him, he was really . . . passionate. I think he'll probably keep playing. The other night I was telling my friend Victor—" I turn my head to look downward at the nothing I'm building. I then realize that I've had the same two Lego bricks in my hand for at least two minutes.

"I heard about Victor," Max says. "What's wrong with him again?"

I shrug and say the longest word I know. "Cardiomyopathy. He's probably gonna die . . . and I really don't want to talk about it right now."

For a moment, Max stops his hands from building. "Are you sure?"

"Yeah," I say. Max goes back to Lego building, but I still keep the same blank stare, holding the same two Lego bricks firmly in my hand. I can't shake the thought of Victor, alone without me.

"So do you think we'll win this week?" He says, snapping me out.

"The Packers?" I say. "I don't know. It'll be a tough game."

But Max is more confident. "I think we'll win, even if it is against the Giants. Still seems weird, though," he says.

"What?"

"The conference championship game, right here in Green Bay. Every football fan alive is gonna be watching. It just seems . . . weird."

"Yeah, I guess it is weird," I say.

And then I realize that the game is much bigger than I'd thought. It's about more than making the winter warmer. It's about our town and our team. And for just one night, our cold, quiet little town will be the biggest city in the whole country.

Max shuffles through a few more Legos. "Plus," he says, "the winner gets to go to the Super Bowl."

19

It's the coldest night of the year. The sky is clear and the moon looks down on the city. I'm safe inside looking out the window, but everyone walking in the street seems to be having second thoughts. It's like the wind is howling at them to leave and look for shelter. Little by little, though, they make their way to the stadium. I think they know this night is too important to turn back.

Some people say that having the home field crowd on your side is no real advantage, that there are way too many other factors that go into who wins and who loses. I don't have any evidence to prove them wrong, but I like to believe that the fans do help. I feel like every fan makes a difference; even us little guys.

"Tyler, can you come in here for a moment?" I hear Victor's dad call out from inside Victor's room. I turn away from the street and join him. Victor is lying on his side with his blanket tucked in beneath him, and his dad is sitting with his elbows on his knees in Victor's desk chair. He's got a thick book open in his hand.

"Take a seat," he says. "In light of the game tonight, I thought I'd read you both a story."

I remember back when I was really young, when Mom or Dad would read to me before I went to sleep, but that hasn't happened in a long time.

I walk over and take a seat on the edge of the bed. The mattress crinkles like the fabric is made of old, dried out paper. The springs groan like they're ready to call it quits.

"All set?" Vic's dad throws on his reading glasses, and I nod.

"Is that book *all* about the Packers?" I say, looking at its thick spine.

"Not exactly, Tyler. But it does have some relevance. It's about a young boy, not much older than you two. His nation was at war with another nation whose people were a lot bigger and stronger. He wanted to join the army to help fight, but they told him he was too small. The boy's name was—"

"David" I say, realizing the book is the Bible.

"David," he repeats. "Have you read the story before?"

"No, but I've heard of it. It's all about a guy slinging rocks at a giant."

"Well, that's part of it. Let's see here . . ." He nudges the reading glasses back up the bridge of his nose and holds the book tight to the dim little lamp.

He reads to us the whole story about David; how no one wanted him, and how he proved all of his family and friends and enemies wrong by defeating the giants with just a sling and a few stones. When he finishes reading, he closes the book and sets it down on Victor's desk.

I ask him, "Do you really believe there were actual giants back then?" He seems caught off guard, so I go on. "I mean, there aren't any giants around anymore, right?"

He rubs his eyes with his thumb and forefinger, wedging the glasses up to his forehead. "Well, there are a few ways you can look at it. The first possibility is that there were real giants. Maybe they all died off, or maybe David and his army killed them all. The second possibility is that it's all made up."

I didn't expect him to be so blunt. I think for a moment, and ask, "Do you think it's real?"

"Yes, I do," he says.

"Really? Real giants?"

But he doesn't seem surprised. He just stares at his thumbs and says, "Giants are interesting creatures. They can be one hundred feet tall, like in the fairy tales you read. Or they can be people just like us. Think of someone really tall you know or you've seen. Maybe they're not as tall as a building in New York, but you could still call them a giant."

181

"So you think those giants were just a bunch of really tall guys?"

I feel the blanket tug beneath me. It looks like Vic is trying to sit up now, so I push myself off the blanket and let him drag it out. Then I look back at his dad. He's thinking, choosing the best words possible, like in a game of Scrabble.

"I don't know. Giants can be other things too, Tyler."

"What do you mean?"

"Well, I think we all have giants in our life. They're the obstacles that stand in our way. They stare down from a hundred feet up and try to intimidate us. They try to make us believe that we're not good enough, not big enough, not strong enough, not brave enough. They try to ruin our faith."

"So you think the giant might be . . . a symbol?"

"I think there are stories—like this one," he pats the book on the cover, "that help us keep the faith that life tries to take away. It doesn't matter if the story is totally accurate, or if it's symbolic. The only thing that matters is how you respond after reading it. You understand?"

"I think so." It really does make a lot more sense when someone is there to explain things to you. "So David stood up to that giant, even though it was tall and standing in his way. It means that we'll have obstacles in our lives, but we can beat them?"

"You're a smart kid, Tyler. It took me a lot longer to figure that one out."

"So that's why you said you believe in giants, then. I guess I do, too."

"Good. I'm glad you said that, because there will be giants that try to tackle you at your worst points in life. It all depends on how you're going to respond to them. I believe in giants, but I believe something else, too. I believe that God provides us every stone we need to fill our sling."

Then Victor speaks. His voice is like a piece of rancid meat, but his words are fresh. "I like that," he says, then he rolls his head onto his pillow, and adds, "We can each slay our own giant."

The wind is belting outside, but it doesn't matter anymore. The whole city is lit up, with a huge beacon of light shooting upward from its center, only a few blocks away.

Now Vic is lying on the living room couch with a pillow propping his head toward the TV. We carried him out here a little while ago. His legs are stretched out to their limits, but there's still enough room for me to sit on the cushion at his feet. His parents are sitting on the floor with their backs to the sofa, and Mom is cuddled alone in the chair across the room.

On TV, the broadcasting gang is huddled around their big desk that is sitting at the corner of the field. They're decked in eighty layers of clothing, trying to keep warm. On the left of the screen, one of the men caresses the game's trophy with a thick winter glove. Through his chattering smile, he reminds everyone that the winner will take the trophy as their first-class ticket to Phoenix where they'll face the undefeated Patriots in the Super Bowl two weeks from tonight.

And then, through all of the excitement, a single whistle is heard.

All of the players take to the field. They're ready to fight. The final battle begins.

Gordon Fisher lets out a deep breath, and watches the air turn into fog and rise into the starry sky.

The Giants are good. They're bigger and stronger, and Gordon knows it. His team has been outplayed this far, and he can feel the cold of his own goal posts breathe down his neck as his team is backed into the thick of their own end zone. More than ever, he's got to remind himself that the others are looking to him for guidance. What they see in him will be what they see in themselves. He makes a cone over his mouth with both his hands and bellows the game plan to his teammates. Each one turns their head to hear him speak.

"We'll hit 'em straight away! If we're winning tonight, we've got to take them down with one swing! Let's go!"

"Break!" His teammates reply. They split into battle formation.

It's early in the second quarter. The Giants hold a 6-0 advantage, but there's plenty of time to play. Gordon knows that the Giants are bigger and stronger, but he also knows they're slower. With the smaller people at his disposal, it means that the Packers will have to be quicker, more agile, and smarter. It means that they'll have to take a leap of faith.

"Green Nineteen!" he yells. "Green Nineteen!" The cadence is all too familiar. As Gordon counts for the snap, he checks his options with Sean wide out to the right. The Giants are in man-to-man coverage, which is what he'd hoped for. He kicks his knee in the air to signal to his center that he's ready.

"Green Nineteen, set, HUT!" The touch of the ball sends an overwhelming symphony of notes through his body. All his life, he knew he'd been born to do this.

He checks to his left, and fakes a toss in the direction of another receiver, and his right foot plants deep into the paint of the one yard line. Now he can see the full field ahead of him. Sean is in the open field down the right. Gordon doesn't hesitate. He bends his arm back like a sling and sends the ball high into the air. He watches it rotate. There's no doubt that he's hit his mark.

The ball lands safely in the hands of his friend. When Gordon realizes that there's nobody ahead of him, he begins chasing the green *DRIVER* jersey the rest of the way to the end zone. God knows he could almost beat him there, he's so happy. The referee at the goal line holds up his arms to signal the touchdown. Gordon throws up his hands in celebration, and he's at Sean's side before he can turn to see. He picks up his receiver and throws him over his shoulder.

"You did it, buddy!"

The living room erupts. I feel like the roof will collapse under the weight of the snow if we shake the apartment any more. The stadium can be heard from a few blocks away, erupting all the same, and I thank God that it doesn't have a roof. My mom jumps off her chair and sweeps me into a hug while Vic's mom and dad share high fives.

While I'm being swung through the air, I'm brought back to earth by someone's voice. It sounds like Vic's dad, but the twirling room is like a roulette, and it could be anybody.

"Okay, okay, calm down everyone." Yep. It's Vic's dad. He sounds exhausted. "We've got a lot of game ahead of us. It's the second quarter and we're only up by one."

Mom practically flings me out of her arms, and I land back on the couch.

"Oh, shut up and let us celebrate," I hear out of Vic's mom. She pushes his shoulder playfully and smiles, and I see Mom curl up into her chair. I turn back to Victor. I lay my hand out for him to give me five, and he slowly lays his hand in mine. Even if that's all the enthusiasm he can muster, I'll take it.

Gordon takes a huff of cold air, and blows it back out in a hot cloud of fog. It's getting late, and the game has lasted longer than any other he's ever played. His arm is exhausted, his lungs hurt from the cold, and his head feels hollow. The wind whips by and stings his face, bursting through the elastic sleeve that's wrapped around it.

It's the coldest night of the year, but there's still work to do. The Packers have been struggling to keep their footing, and trail the Giants 20-17. Gordon takes another breath. With each passing tick in the fourth quarter, the clock brings him closer to his final decision.

The lights and the fans and his teammates all beam down around him. He feels like the world is spinning in circles. He wishes he could close his eyes and shed them all away again, but the thumping of his heart would find him there, and he still would not be alone.

"We've got this," he says in the huddle. Each one of his words is labored, but he presses on. "We've made it this far. I don't want to see anyone giving up. You hear me?" He looks around to his ten other teammates. Each one wears a face of determination.

"Alright, let's go." Gordon claps his hands together and winces as they both sting.

"Break!" The team responds.

Gordon takes his position behind the center. His running back lines up at his side. He can see the end zone, and his three receivers are spread out wide, yearning to get there. Wasting no time, he barks out the cadence.

"Green Nineteen! Green Nineteen, set, HUT!"

He steps back into the pocket and immediately turns to his receivers, but they're all covered. He fakes to his left, but nobody on the defense is fooled. A Giants' defender swoops around the line and closes in from behind. Gordon's once hollow head is now swimming with choices. Take the tackle. Throw it away. Throw it to the ground. Thread it to Sean. Tuck the ball and run.

Then he sees Sean break free. Gordon takes a step forward, missing the defender by the swoop of an arm. He launches the ball down the left side of the field and prays for delivery. All of the previous passes lingered in the air for centuries, as if they were each a precious work of art hanging there to be admired, but this one is over a lot quicker.

The ball is snagged out of the air by a Giant. The man in the blue jersey takes the ball into his chest and starts running the opposite way before he's roped to the ground by Gordon's teammate.

Gordon turns away and pulls off his chinstrap. He closes his eyes and tilts his head to the sky.

We were so close.

The crowd roars. Gordon's heart is pierced by the sound he knew was coming and sinks to the bottom of his gut. But then he listens. They aren't yells—they're cheers. He flicks his eyes open and turns back around. His own running back is dancing above the toppled Giant, waving the ball high in his hand. The referee signals first down for the Packers.

We got the ball back?

Gordon looks up to the video screen and watches the replay. Before the defender falls to the ground, his running back rips his arms apart and steals the ball back. Gordon's heart latches to its one last remaining thread and climbs back up to his chest with a renewed sense of faith.

We've got a game to play.

Gordon sifts through the other players on the way back to the huddle, and touches his teammate on the shoulder.

"Where'd you learn to strip the ball like that?" He says.

"I'm not a running back," he says, "I'm a football player."

Gordon gives him a manly pat on the backside, and they both go into the huddle. Four plays later, their kicker comes onto the field and boots a 37-yard field goal to tie the game.

The grown-ups cheer when the ball goes through the goalposts, but I'm still gripping at the arm of the couch. My stomach feels like it's on one of those twister rides at a carnival, spinning around and around and flipping upside down. Mom is tucked with a small blanket held up to her face like she's bracing for impact. Vic's mom and dad are stuck to the TV like a moth to light. Vic hasn't moved at all, and the only reassuring sign is that the blanket over him is hovering up and down with each breath.

Only four seconds are left and the game is still tied, but the Giants have moved the ball all the way down to the 18-yard line, and now their kicker is preparing for a field goal in the shadows of our goal posts. It's a chip shot.

It feels like the pit of my stomach wants out, like my whole body is rejecting something that I didn't even eat. The entire city of Green Bay is the same. It's weird how silent everyone gets when there's nothing left to do but watch.

The ball is snapped. The kick is up. It misses, wide to the left.

The grown-ups jump out of their seats and start hugging each other in celebration. I give the grown-ups a smile, but I feel less like them and more like Victor. I don't think I could manage to stand up if I tried. My heart keeps pounding and I close my eyes to try to relax.

The game is still tied, and it's going into overtime. That's where everything starts over again. You get a new game and a clean slate. There's just one new rule—the first team to score wins.

Gordon Fisher hands the ball off to his running back on the first play of overtime. As he does, he watches him become lost in a pile of green and blue. The play was humble one, and it gained only a few yards. But then again, it was never intended to be brilliant. It was only ever intended to be the preamble to greatness.

It's the second play that will prove to be the one that everyone remembers.

His teammates surround him. With unmatched authority, he shouts out the game plan, telling each where to go and what to do. They split into battle formation. Each will face his own giant alone, but together they will fight as one team.

"Green nineteen!" He shouts.

"Green nineteen!"

Now his heart beats in rhythm. It's slow, calm. There's nothing left but him and the path ahead.

"Set, hut!"

It all returns. Gordon takes the ball in hand from his center, knowing full well that every action has a consequence. He takes a fraction of a second to think about the past two decades, and it seems humbling that this is what he has to show for it. All the decisions he's made in his entire career—all the consequences—have led to him standing right here on the north end of Lambeau Field. Soon he might not be standing here. Maybe he will be or maybe he won't, because another fraction of a second will cause another decision that will cause another consequence.

That fraction of a second passes by. He drops back a few yards, and his linemen begin their attempt to stave off the Giants defense. No longer is he thinking about his past. He's thinking about his present. He checks his first option: Sean. But he's being covered step-for-step down field by his cornerback. Gordon decides against it for now—he'll check back on him later. A Giants' defensive tackle loops around back, and Gordon dodges forward. He's now fully encircled by his teammates. He's counting on them, trusting that each one will be able to slay his own Giant.

Another fraction of a second passes, and his running back breaks into the open field. Gordon chooses not to throw to him, knowing full well that every action has a consequence. Sean cuts back outside at the 45-yard line, trying to shed his defender off the route. Another fraction of a second passes, and Gordon needs to make a decision. His arm bends back like a sling, and he swings it forward knowing full well that every action has a consequence.

As the ball floats through the two decades it took to get there, Gordon takes a split second to ponder his career and his life. There were so many decisions, and so many consequences. Perhaps this will be the final decision. Perhaps there will be one more. All he knows is that he can never have this one back. The ball revolves unbelievably slowly. It's a clock, and the laces are the second hand, slowly but gradually ticking away and eating the little amount of time each person has left. After what seems like an eternity trapped in this sublime universe, the air beneath the ball shatters and it drops clean out of the sky. Gordon is no longer thinking about the present. He is thinking about the future.

Every action has a consequence, and because of that, there is one more decision to make. He starts chasing the ball. Chasing the path that he has never taken before. He sinks his foot deep into the turf so that it will never be forgotten. He crosses the battlefield, and on the horizon he can see what true glory really means.

The ball is intercepted. It doesn't matter. He knew it the whole time, and the whole time he knew that there would be one more decision. The words motivated him. The words made an impact in him and changed him in a way that he knew he could never determine. *You've gotta put everything on the line, risk every ounce of your life to make it happen. You've got nothing else to lose.*

He ducks his shoulder and lunges forward, colliding with every single triumph and every single heartbreak that brought him here tonight. The stress that has dissatisfied him for years erupts. Right then, there is no game and no stadium and no Green Bay and no Earth. There is only pure existence, pure light. It is warm, calming, and beautiful.

An instant later, he lands, and in landing, he realizes that there must be Earth, and there must be life, and there must be a game.

The game.

All he can see now is the turf below his facemask. His ears are ringing, and he can barely hear himself ask, "What happened?" He turns his head to see that there's no one else around to hear him anyway. Everyone else is piled together at the other end of the field and the fans are bouncing on their feet.

The stadium screen shows the replay of Gordon lunging into the stomach of the Giants' defender. The ball pops free from his hands, and Sean scoops it off the ground and starts running down the sideline.

Gordon's eyes burst wide. He watches the legs of his friend on the screen, racing and spinning so fast that they look like wheels. At the 10-yard line, the Giant's safety catches up to him and swings his fist at his right arm. Sean stumbles but holds onto the ball, and falls to the ground at the 5-yard line.

"Gordon! Gordon, get up, we've gotta get you off the field!" Gordon's attention snaps away from the screen. For a moment, it had felt like he was living up there instead. The hand of a coach touches him on the back. "Gordon, you alright?"

"Yeah." Gordon pushes himself into a sit. There's a sharp pain in his shoulder and he clutches it without thinking.

"You're sure?"

"Yeah, I'm fine."

"Okay, good, now get off the field."

"Wha—but I've gotta go play!"

"Gordon, you just *did* play! That was amazing! Now get yourself off the field before we get a penalty, and it all goes for nothing!"

Gordon realizes that all the time he spent watching the screen, the field goal team was racing onto the field to put the game away. He hesitates for a moment, wishing he could go down and take the snap, but then a wave of calmness rushes over him.

I just did play. That was amazing. I feel amazing.

He scrambles to his feet and gets off the field. Seconds later, the ball is snapped and the kicker puts it straight through the goal posts. The final play is over so quickly that Gordon wonders if it ever even happened. It's weird. The field goal seemed to take no time at all, but the play before it took an eternity.

"Did you see that?" I jump so high I almost take the roof off by myself. My words are loud, but they're lost among the other screams in the room. All the grown-ups are on their feet, and my mom runs over to hug me again.

"We did it!" she shouts.

"No, the play before!" My mouth is muffled by the grip of her arms. I try to get it out, but no one can hear me. I twist and push, but it only makes her think I want to hug her tighter. I do. I do want to hug her tighter but not right now because there's something else. That last play. The one before the field goal.

I throw my weight against her and finally break free. She thinks it's all in celebration. This is the greatest time ever. I think. No, wait, maybe I'm wrong. Maybe I need to see it one more time. Maybe my mind was playing tricks on me and it was really just a crazy fantasy I had. I lean down next to the couch. Victor is lying there about as ecstatic as a sack of flour.

"Vic, you saw that play, didn't you?" I press my face close to hear him over the others.

"Yeah, we won the game," his voice comes through the blanket tucked over his mouth.

"No, no, no, the play before it! You saw how Gordon tackled that guy and made him drop the ball. That was you, Vic! That was you!"

For the first time in a month, I see a flicker that hadn't been there before. It's like the lights of the room started a flame within his eyes. A flame that just might burn bright enough to understand what I mean. "C'mon, Vic. I know you know."

By now, the others have noticed that we're not celebrating with them. They've all stopped in their tracks and now face me and Victor, with the celebration still strong in the background. I stand up and turn to them.

"What's wrong?" Mom asks.

"There's nothing wrong! We won the game! And it was Victor who did it!"

Now they're dead silent. It hurts, because I don't know how to explain what I mean. "A few months ago, when we were in the locker room after the game, Victor told Gordon to do that!"

"To do what?" says Mom.

"To tackle him, just like he did there! To make him fumble! Victor told him in the locker room when we went to the game!" They all laugh. They think it's cute, but their laughter makes me shake.

"Tyler, we didn't even know this game was happening until we won last week. How could you have known back in

October?" Someone says it, but I really don't care who it was. I just want to explain myself.

"No, that's not what I mean! I mean that Victor told him to try hard and give it everything he has, or . . . or something like that! I don't know, I just know that it happened!" I feel my body start to sweat, like I'm under a big heat lamp. I can tell that they don't believe a word of it. Why don't they believe it? Are my words so unbelievable? Is it impossible that it was Victor's words that changed him? Is it impossible that he had some courage and defended his friend? Is it impossible to believe that he stood up to one of the biggest giants in his life and told him what to do?

But the grown-ups have lost interest, and now they're watching the TV. Players are hugging and celebrating. People are passing out shirts and hats that say *Super Bowl*. Vic is still looking at me though. I kneel back down and speak right into his ear. "Vic, you know it and I know it. That's all that matters, okay?"

He doesn't speak. He doesn't even move his head.

"You *do* believe it, don't you Vic?"

He turns his eyes away from mine. He's looking at nothing. "I don't know," he says, "It happened pretty fast. It's hard to tell."

My lip starts to shake but I don't know why, and I suddenly feel very alone.

"Vic, don't say that."

"I mean, it was a long time ago. Don't you think he'd have forgotten what I said by now?"

"No!" I say the words through my teeth, and I grab his head with both my hands. "Vic, he remembers." But when I say those words, it's like they become clear to me as well. There's no way he'd remember.

I turn around, and slowly, I put my back against the sofa. The trophy ceremony is running on the TV and I put my eyes to the screen, but I don't really pay attention. I sit there and think about how blurry everything is. Not with my eyes, but in life. I realize that Vic is right. A lot of things come into play that make you do what you do. What's truly impossible is determining which ones had the biggest impact. There's no way to tell. There's no way to know.

They've got a stage with a podium set up on the field. One of the guys from the broadcasting team is up there with a microphone, and he's got the conference championship trophy in his hand. He's interviewing the coach, but whatever words they're saying float right by me. Then the coach backs away from the microphone, and the broadcaster beckons Gordon Fisher up on the stage.

"Gordon!" he says. "I've got a cup of hot cocoa waiting inside for me, so what do you say we make this quick?" I can hear the crowd laugh, and it puts a smile on Gordon's face. The man goes on. "Tell us how it feels to be going back to the big game after, what, how many years?"

"Too many to count," Gordon says. The words echo around the stadium, and I can hear the muffled remains far outside the window. "It feels good. I'm so proud of my guys and our coaches, and the fans. They deserve all the credit." The crowd roars in response.

The man smiles, and says, "Gordon, tell us about that last play there. What was going through your mind when you made that tackle?"

"Well, to tell you the truth, not a lot. I hit the guy, then I hit the ground. He dropped the ball, so I guess it worked pretty well."

I sit in the living room surrounded by the people I love, but I feel a million miles away from anything and everything. There's a pain in my heart. Something that's never been there before. When I see the man on the screen, I see him the same way I did before. He's a shadow. His eyes look directly at me—directly into me. They kill me.

But all I hear is laughter.

"I'll say it worked well!" The broadcaster bellows into the microphone. The crowd roars in applause, and he goes on, "Well, congratulations, Gordon. You earned it. Now, I'd tell you to go ahead and throw on that new hat of yours, but, well, it looks like it got put through a shredder. You might want to go grab a different one."

"Nah, that's okay. This is my handy work," he says, "and I like it just fine."

He lifts the hat up and then swivels it down onto his head in one swift motion, but that one swift motion takes more than a million eternities, and the entire world stands still. I don't mean that the world is frozen, or that the world is sad. I mean the exact opposite. I mean that there is no more such thing as cold, and there is no more such thing as sad, and there's no more suffering or hating or hurting or darkness. In that one swift motion, with that one beautiful, flawless, jagged-brimmed hat, the entire world is changed.

Victor's parents drop to their knees. I'd say they're in disbelief, but with what we just saw with our very own eyes, it's impossible not to believe.

"What is it?" Mom says, and that's when I realize that she doesn't understand.

"Mom, that's Victor's hat!"

"What? Where?"

"Right there!" I point at the screen, and I'm on my feet now. "That's Victor's hat on Gordon's head!"

"That's Victor's hat?"

"No, no it's not Victor's hat, but he's got one just like it with the brim all chopped up and it was me who chopped it up, but that was a long time ago, and he left it in the locker room when we saw Gordon after the game, and he must've picked it up and now he must've cut the same pattern into his own hat AND THAT MEANS THAT HE REMEMBERED WHAT VICTOR SAID! I TOLD YOU! I TOLD YOU IT WAS VICTOR!" I shout. I'm jumping up and down, and my heart is racing. I still can't tell if I believe it myself, but that's not important, because it's true.

Mom stands there with a confused face. She still doesn't get it, does she?

"Here, Mom," I say, "I'll show you! Victor, your hat's in your room, right?" I turn to Victor and then I realize his blanket is empty. We all look around the room, and then a door slams in the hallway.

"Victor!" I run to the door and try to open it up, but it's been locked or wedged closed or something cause the knob turns but the door won't open. "Victor! Victor open up, I need you out here right now!"

Soon his parents are right behind me, and they're knocking on the door just as loud as I am.

"Victor! Are you alright?" says his dad. No response comes, but for how soft his voice is we probably couldn't hear him over the banging on the door.

"Victor, we need you to come out right now!" his mom shouts. "Victor!"

I peer under the crack in the door and see the shadow of something scoot across the floor, and I think it's a chair. The door falls open and his parents stumble over the doorway. Victor is kneeled down on the floor, and his mom reaches down to scoop him up. Then everything slows down and gets real quiet. Not even the stadium can be heard anymore. The city is resting.

"Victor, you're okay. You're okay," his mom says in a hushed voice. She starts stroking his hair and rocking him from side to side like a baby.

We all wait there for a half hour. Nobody moves. We're all okay together. Everything is okay.

19

Victor once told me he thought I could win the race. But just like everything else he told me, it took some time for me to start believing him. When I ended up losing the race, I began to wonder if he really believed in me, or if he was just trying to make me feel better. I began to lose confidence in myself. But then Victor showed me that the race wasn't what was important.

I don't know if it really makes any sense, but now I feel like Victor's in a race. This time he's the one that needs encouragement, and I'm the one that needs to help him. There's just one problem. I can't help him, because I know he's going to lose.

I see Victor on the hospital bed. He's pale and he's blue. He looks like he's almost gone now. His heart is giving out on him, and I want to help, but I know I can't. There's nothing anyone can do anymore.

I walk up to his side. "Vic," I say. "Hey, Vic."

I turn away the instant I speak. Mom is right behind me. I dig my face into the flap of her jacket.

"Victor, there's someone here to see you." I can't see, but I can tell it's his mom's voice. Both his parents are by his bedside. She says the words like he's a small child and can't understand well. Like he's not even Victor anymore. I can't stand that thought. Can I still talk to him like he's my friend, or is he something completely different now?

I peel back the flap of Mom's jacket. The lights in the hospital are much brighter than the ones at Victor's home, but they're less comfortable too. It's like they're trying to expose me. I wish I could stay hidden, but I know I can't.

"Hey Victor," I say again. I touch his hand, and I can tell he's listening. It feels like the other night, sitting in his bedroom and hearing a story. Now it's my turn to tell a story.

"Vic, I—I don't know if you remember this," I stop to wipe a stream of water and grime from my face and onto my sleeve. My arm starts to shiver from the cold, and then my whole body starts to shiver. "There—there was this one time in my garage when we were both building the racer together. It was the first time I felt afraid that you were gonna die. I said that I didn't want to work on the racer anymore because I felt like the race didn't matter. But you kept on working. You didn't even say a word. You just kept on working.

"Well, Vic, I—" The words are there, but they're scrambling to leave my throat like they're all jammed in a doorway. I realize at that moment that words and actions go together, and that it would be impossible to keep on talking like I am right now.

I bend over and bury my head into the pillow beside him. I sweep his fragile body into a warm hug, and God knows he needs it; he's so cold. I shiver even more, and I worry that I'll shiver so hard that I'll break him.

"Vic. You gotta hear me. I never wanted to stop. I hate this. I HATE THIS SO MUCH!" I cry tears that are so strong that they melt my face down into his pillow, and I don't know if there's even anything to cry out of anymore. The motionless figure in my arms is the same one that made me strong and brave. I can't let him die like this. The world needs him. His work isn't over yet. It doesn't make any sense.

Mom comes over and touches me on the shoulder. I feel her hand bobbing up and down to the beat of my lungs. I don't want any of this. If I could make it stop I would, but I can't.

I force myself to stop sobbing because I need to let him know.

"Vic, I need you to hear something that I thought of. It's something that I know you'll like. It's about meaning.

"You see, you can try to get things in life that will make you happy, but when it's all over, those things don't matter. You can't take them with you, so you leave them behind and they rot away. But what does have meaning is the way you've changed other people's lives. And you changed my life. You made me a better person. Someday down the line, I'll turn around and pass that on to others, and I'll change their lives too, and then they'll turn around and do the same thing."

I clutch his hand tighter. I'm no longer afraid of breaking him because his spirit is the only thing that matters.

"I guess what I mean to say is that you've changed the world already. You're just a kid, but you've changed the world. And you've given me the courage and strength to do it too."

His body doesn't reply.

"We're gonna be alright," I go on. "We're going to miss you. I'm going to miss you. And I wish you'd stay here to—to keep me company, and—" I wipe a tear away and my voice starts to tremble,"—and to keep teaching me stuff. But I know we'll be alright at the same time, cause you've already taught us so much."

I squeeze him tighter, and I feel him squeeze back. For a second, his body feels warm. For just one second, we're back on top of the hill. The snow is surrounding us and the wind is whipping in our faces, and as the racer begins to pick up speed, there's no more fear. It's completely lost in the flakes of snow, and everything is okay.

It's raining in January that day as Mom and I leave the hospital. There are some spots on the ground where you can see bits of grass poking through the snow and rain, reaching toward the sky. In other places, there are patches of dirt and groups of stones exposed. I remember what Victor's dad said about God providing us with stones for our sling. I hope he's right.

Eventually, Victor's parents and I will start working on the Victory Foundation again. I don't know how long it will be until then, but I look forward to the day. Victor's parents said they wanted to. They said they believed that their son had started something good.

When I think about it, that's really who Victor was in life. He was a starter. A pusher. He pushed everyone he knew in the right direction, and that's because he knew it was the right thing to do.

But most of all, he taught me the two most important lessons I know: you're never too young to make a difference, and it's never too late to change the world.

Mom and I pull into the back parking lot of Victor's apartment. I guess it's kind of ours now, too, even if nobody says it out loud. For a few moments, the engine rumbles softly through the pavement. Then Mom turns the car off, and there are only raindrops on the windshield.

"Come here," Mom says. I'm sitting in the passenger seat, but I unbuckle my seatbelt and scoot over into her arms. "You're okay, Tyler. You're okay. Don't worry, just let it all out. Mom's here. You're okay."

I wrap my arms tight around her waist, and now it's like we're each other's seatbelt. The rain beats down on the world outside, but for now, in here, it can't touch us.

After half an hour, the rain gets softer but the sky stays gray. Mom and I quietly go inside.

I go into Victor's room and close the door. There's a smell that I'd forgotten existed. It's stale and rotten, but at the same time it smells like a living, breathing Victor. I look around at everything in his room.

There's his desk. His dad's Bible is still resting on the corner where he left it. The autographed football with everyone's name on it is just inches away. Then there's the hat. I look at it. The hat that changed the world. It's old and faded, but the signatures still shine.

There's his window. I helped him escape the prison of his room one night by pelting that window with snowballs. The window is small, but it always gave him a way out. It gave him light.

I look down at the bed. Is it my bed now? I don't know what's ahead, but we might be staying here for a long time while Dad sorts everything out. They say he's getting help right now, and that one day we might be a family again. I think I'd like that, but not right away.

For now I'm happy living here. I'm happy letting Victor's family take care of us, just like we did for them when they lost their home. Most of all, I'm happy living here because it's where I feel comfy. The roof might be small, but the people below it love each other. Like a light shining down and keeping us all warm.

I hop up onto the corner of the mattress. It's crusty, and there's a crinkling sound coming from underneath. I reach down and pull out a sheet of paper. It's dry, wrinkled and ripped, like it's been sitting there longer than the bed sheets, even. I study the front and back, and run my finger over the words:

Things I want to do before I die.

I can tell right away that it's Victor's handwriting. The things in the list give it away even more. At the bottom is an empty checkbox. And the words next to it tear me to shreds.

Win the race with Tyler.

It was one of his last wishes, and we failed.

I know he would tell me that the race was never important, but I feel like I let him down. I don't know if that feeling will ever go away.

I look at the rest of the list. *Eat an entire box of Oreos. Go skydiving. Go skateboarding on the moon.* I run my finger past each entry, and each one is like a part of Victor. I start to cry more, and then more. I realize this is the biggest memory in this room. His joke side, his serious side, and his biggest, craziest dreams. He's all here.

Then I come to the top of the list and read the first entry.

Take the Packers to the Super Bowl.

There's a checkmark in the box to the left. I look over to the hat on his desk. The hat that changed the world. This is what he was doing when he locked us out of his room last night.

I look back to the list, and study the checkmark that he made. It means he did the impossible. It means he made a difference, even though he didn't know it at the time. I stare at the words, the *true* words, *Take the Packers to the Super Bowl.*

I speak to Victor out loud. "You did it."

I clutch the paper close to my chest. I know it's not the same as hugging Victor, but it's close. The checkmark means that he held the same paper just a little bit ago. It means the memory of him is still here.

I look one more time around the room, at all the memories that make Victor still living and breathing around me. I'm drawn one more time to the hat that changed the world. I've seen the signatures a million times, but I never took the time to study them. I walk over to the desk and set the list down right next to the marker.

I take the hat in my hand and swivel it around to Sean's signature. There are some letters and numbers beneath it. I don't recognize what they mean, but I recognize where they come from. I reach over and grab the Bible sitting on the edge of the desk.

I peel the book open and flip through it until I find the passage in the signature. I read it quietly in my mind.

I have fought the good fight, I have finished the race, I have kept the faith.

My eyes skip back to the beginning, and I read it again. When I'm finished I read it a third time and a fourth time and so many times that I lose count.

We have fought the good fight.

We have finished the race.

We have kept the faith.

Together, Victor, we built each other up, and we made each other better. I'll always remember you for fighting the good fight and for keeping the faith. But I'll remember you most for staying in the race until the very end.

I grab the marker and pop off the cap. I slide the list back in front of me, and in one swift motion, I make a checkmark through the box at the bottom of the page. It's so satisfying. It's so beautiful. *Win the race with Tyler.* I speak to him one last time.

"We did it."

POSTGAME:
KEEPING THE LIGHT ON

Before being taken here, I remember Mom telling me not to worry about them—about how sad they'll be or about how much money they'll make or any of that. She said money will come with work and work will come with time, but neither of those things are important in the end.

I always thought it was neat that Mom is an electrician. What gets me most is how she always keeps the light burning, even if it's burning so dim that you can hardly see. Through everything, through all the crap I gave her, she still tried to keep the light burning inside of me.

Right now I can feel the light's presence, even though I don't know where it's coming from. There's a deep, dense fog, but through it all I can still tell exactly where I am. I'm standing on the edge of glory. Tyler was right about everything.

"Victor," I hear my name from somewhere just beyond where I can see. From the fog, a figure appears on a bench and I recognize the large man.

"Gordon?" I ask. As the fog starts to clear, I can tell he's waiting for me over by his locker stall, just like he did some long time ago. He's wearing the same hat I saw him wear on the TV. The words *Super Bowl* burst off of the front, and the brim is hacked to shredded perfection. He's wearing his jersey, too, but I'm a little disappointed when I see the color. When Tyler told me about Heaven, he told me the angel would be wearing a white Packer jersey, but Gordon is wearing a green one.

Finally I ask, "Gordon, are you the angel?"

His face turns to a smile and he shakes his head. "No, Victor. They don't let guys like us do things like that, at least not yet. You've gotta earn the right."

"Well, then what *are* you doing here?"

"I needed to talk to you before you went away."

"Oh."

He motions for me to come sit next to him on the bench. I take a seat and then look deep into his eyes.

"Are you real?" I say.

Again he replies with a smile on his face. "I'm not pretend, if that's what you're asking."

I turn to look ahead of me, though not really at anything in particular. The bench is too high for my feet to reach the floor, so I start swinging them back and forth. That's when I realize that I'm already wearing shoes. Clothes and pads too. It's like I'm suited up for a football game.

I turn back to Gordon. "So what did you need to talk to me for?"

"I wanted to know if you saw the game."

"Yeah, I saw it."

"And afterward?"

"I saw that too."

"So . . ." He pauses and leaves the word hanging in the air. ". . . am I forgiven?"

I take my time answering. I look into his honest eyes, and I glance upward to study the cuts in his hat one more time. Then I say, "Yeah, it's no big deal."

"Good," he says. "I guess I needed to know that you got the message." He turns away and stares at his hands, which are folded between his knees. "I'm sorry I was mean to you. There wasn't any reason for it, I just—"

"It's okay. I know you didn't mean to."

He nods his head and then turns around to the lockers. "So, you gonna throw that thing on, or what?" He points at the locker next to his. I check behind me and notice that there's a jersey hanging from a hook inside, and it's got my name on it. But not my last name. It just says VICTOR in all capitals.

I turn back. "Shouldn't I wait until the angel gets here?"

"I'm sure the angel won't mind. Besides, nothing passes the time like a game of catch." He waves his hand in the air and a wisp of fog forms into a football. He takes it by the threads and stands up. "What do you say?"

I stand up too. I walk over and take the jersey off its hook, then throw it on. I step out into the center of the locker room. Most of the fog is gone, but as I look around the room, it's still impossible to tell where the light is coming from. We start throwing the ball back and forth.

"So do you think you'll win the Super Bowl?" I ask.

"Hah. I don't know. You got any more pointers for me that could help?"

"Sorry. I'm fresh out."

Gordon smiles. "I think it doesn't much matter. It's just a game, to be honest."

"Yeah, that's true. So then what are you gonna do after the game?"

"What do you mean?"

"You know. Are you gonna retire?"

Gordon catches one of my throws and brings the ball to his side. He considers his answer. "I don't know that either. Do you think I should?"

I laugh. "I'm not brave enough to answer that right now."

He laughs too. "I guess that's fair. People always think I'm drawing out the decision just to get attention. But I'm really just taking as much time as I can to weigh it all out. Every action has a consequence, you know. I just don't want to make the wrong decision." When he says decision, he throws the ball again and we continue going back and forth.

"I hear you," I say. "I think there are also some decisions where neither one is the wrong one. If you keep the faith, you'll be okay."

"That's good. I like that." He catches the ball and looks to his right. I follow his gaze, and I realize that the time has finally come. A large figure waits in the fog.

"Looks like your angel is here. You'd better get going now."

"Thanks," I say, "Thanks for coming, thanks for talking, and thanks for playing catch."

"You got it. Oh, and don't forget your helmet." He points back to my locker. I must have missed it. I walk back over and take the helmet off the hook, but once it's in my hands I realize that it's not my helmet at all. It's the hat that changed the world. I look at the two signatures—Sean's and Gordon's—which glisten by the light that's beginning to overtake the fog. I turn around with the hat in my hands and walk back to the center of the room.

"Here," I say, and I hold the hat up to Gordon. "It's a trade. Yours for mine."

"Are you *sure*?" he says.

"Yeah, I'm sure. Like I said; two options and neither one is wrong. I want you to have this one."

Gordon takes the hat from me as though he knew it would be this way all along. He pulls off the *Super Bowl* hat by the jagged brim and clumsily stuffs it onto my head. I straighten it out and then I look back into his eyes.

"I gotta go," I say.

"I know. You'll be fine. You're in good hands." Gordon looks at the figure behind me. He smiles and waves to him, as though he's an old friend.

I turn to meet him too. The fog is completely gone now, and the figure is standing in the doorway with his hand offered out in my direction. I see that he's wearing a Packer jersey, too—a beautiful, shining *WHITE* jersey. I walk to him and take his hand. He tells me that everything is okay. We turn to face the doorway, and I can see that the tunnel leads down to the field. I can hear the fans now—thousands, maybe millions of them. They're waiting for me.

The angel takes the first step, and I follow soon after. We start out slow, but ever so slowly, we begin to pick up speed. At last, I can see where the light is coming from. It's coming from the field at the other end of the tunnel—coming from the lights that flood the stadium in warmth. The closer I get, the more I can feel the warmth of the lights spreading throughout my entire body. I begin to realize that it was always about the lights. It was always about searching for the warmth that they give us. At the end of this tunnel that leads us into glory, the eternal warmth awaits.

We're running fast now, and the crowd is roaring. They're ready for me. As we reach the end, I finally realize that the lights were the most important part all along.

And I think she would be happy for me to know that.

ACKNOWLEDGMENTS

Together, we build each other up, and for that reason, I want to say thank you:

To my parents for encouraging me to stick with it. For reading my first rough copies, and for being patient while I wrote. For helping me emotionally and at times economically, because you wanted me to succeed. To Andrew, who knows what it means to be good and true, and who inspires me every day, more than any other person in the whole world. To Mama Marsha, for being a strong leader, and for bringing the lights to Lambeau Field.

To my friends who encouraged me, and didn't bother me too much when I stayed in to write while you were all out. To my guys and former roommates, Kris Ross, Landon Burlingham, Phil McDaniel, Max Hayes, Ezra Frater, Jake Brockmann, Matt Olson, Troy Beyer, and the others who I mention below. To Elliott Martinson, for being my first friend and first audience to all the ridiculous stories I wrote as a kid, and for being the one who went outside in the blizzard to throw the football with me, even when it was so dark that we couldn't see the ball. To Caleb Krueger, for encouraging me to keep writing. To Mike Seitz, for being a true friend, and a genuine blessing to the world. To Nick Wipperfurth and Chris Lynch, for continuing to ask me about the book, and being genuinely interested in the project. To Jeff Way and Paul van der Salm, for being my best friends and great encouragers. To Scott Cook for being a trusted friend and mentor, and advising me on publication and marketing strategies.

To Jess Kibler, for your thorough and dedicated read-through, and immensely helpful feedback on content. To Frannie Sprouls for your rigorous work and dedication to proofreading and editing. To Randy Nelson and Jared Lemon for dedicating your time and reading through the way-too-long first draft, and Randy for giving another shot at the final draft. You guys rock! To the Cheeseheads at /r/greenbaypackers who helped and gave feedback. To Alex Immendorf, for giving poignant and helpful feedback as well. To Allison Julander for reading, critiquing, and most importantly, inspiring me to keep going. To Taylor Kalish, for your very helpful feedback, and for being an inspiration, an academic, a good friend, and one of the best people I know. Now it's your turn!

To my teachers. To Mrs. Hoyt, for being the first one who saw me as a writer and a creator, and for reading the very first story I ever wrote in 4th grade, about an underdog peewee football team. To Mrs. Rendler, for believing and convincing me that I would be an entertainer. To Mrs. Steffen for letting us share our stories in class, and believing without a doubt that I would be a writer. I always believed it too, but before you, it was a dream. To Carmen Manning, for being my lifeline, friend, and navigator of life! To teachers everywhere, please understand this and live it every day; The smallest gesture can make a whole world of difference.

To the Packers, for being my favorite team, but most of all, for giving us all something to look forward to during the most brutal winter months. For giving us a reason to squeeze together on the living room couch and warm each other up, and to smile, laugh, cry, cheer, and truly feel that we are a part of something great.

To children everywhere who stick up for their friends, even when it's the hard thing to do. To children who stay by their friend's side when they feel abandoned. To children who encourage one another, because they want to do good for the world. To all children, know this; You are never too young to make a difference. To all grown-ups, know this; It is never too late to change the world.

To anyone who gives their time or money to a great

cause—even when they don't see results or recognition—because they believe in the power of good.

To anyone who has lost someone close, but still knows that their influence will last a lifetime.

And lastly, to all friends who truly care, because friends are the one thing that makes life worth living.

ABOUT THE AUTHOR

MATTHEW NEBEL wrote his first work of fiction when he was ten years old, a 13-page story about a boy and his football team trying to win the city championship. Ever since then, he has had a deep passion for influencing the world in a positive way through storytelling. *Football in Heaven* was written mostly during his time at the University of Wisconsin-Eau Claire, where he studied English and Spanish Education. Born and raised in Wisconsin, his family owns one share of Green Bay Packers, Inc. This is his first novel.

MAKE A DIFFERENCE

A portion of the proceeds from *Football in Heaven* will be donated to non-profit charities that focus on childhood illness in both Wisconsin and the Pacific Northwest. For more information, visit www.FootballinHeaven.com.